PRAISE FOR
South on Highland

"A very cool debut from a very cool writer. *South on Highland* belongs to a special literary tradition: the kind of book that kids will steal from each other."

—B. J. Novak, bestselling author of *One More Thing*
and *Book with No Pictures*

"A humorous work of provocative nostalgia. Liana Maeby has written *Less Than Zero* for the emoji generation."

—Jason Reitman, director of *Juno* and *Up in the Air*

"Liana Maeby has a serious way with words. *South on Highland* is a delightful, Adderall-fueled romp through Hollywood indulgence."

—Ariel Schrag, author of *Adam*

"Hilarious and gut wrenching, both by turns and sometimes simultaneously. If this world is familiar to you, you'll instantly fall into its authentic groove. If it's foreign, you'll find no tour guide more witty, more soulful, or more full of perception than the immensely talented Liana Maeby."

—Rian Johnson, writer and director of *Brick* and *Looper*

"Liana Maeby has crafted a magic trick of a novel—profane and funny and devastating, and above all, fun as hell. As sexy and silly, dangerous and creepy as Jim Morrison's leather pants, *South on Highland* does what the best drug novels do: make one both deeply aware of the insidious cost of drug addiction, and want to go get super wasted."

—Stephen Falk, creator of *You're the Worst* on FX

"Don't say no to Maeby, say yes to *South on Highland.* If the madness and kaleidoscope values that make up life in LA could be captured in a book, it would have to be in the format hilariously realized in this incredible book. So funny because it's so real, so real because it's so horrifying, Liana Maeby has written the ultimate eulogy to American culture at its logical and geographic endpoint."

—Richard Rushfield, editor-in-chief of HitFix
and author of *Don't Follow Me, I'm Lost*

"Liana Maeby makes possibly dying from a head wound on the floor of a millionaire's bathroom funnier than it has any right to be. *South on Highland* is fast, thrilling, and incredibly clever."

—Kevin Seccia, author of *Punching Tom Hanks*

SOUTH ON HIGHLAND

SOUTH ON HIGHLAND

a novel

LIANA MAEBY

Text copyright © 2015 Liana Maeby

Published by Little A, New York

www.apub.com

Amazon, the Amazon logo, and Little A are trademarks of Amazon.com, Inc., or its affiliates.

ISBN-13: 9781477829882
ISBN-10: 1477829881

Cover design by Adil Dara

Library of Congress Control Number: 2014921615

Printed in the United States of America

For Carol, my mother, the strongest and the best person, to whom I owe everything.

PROLOGUE

The pills spilled to the ground like debris from a tornado, landing in various wet spots around the toilet. No, they tumbled out like a wintry mix: Klonopin hail, OxyContin rain, Vicodin snow. No, like that moment on the 101, somewhere around Barham, when accident traffic suddenly unclogs and the cars all shoot forward at once.

I was supposed to be looking for the afikomen at Jerry Weinbach's Passover seder, but instead, I raided the master bathroom for the pills I assumed Jerry's wife, Miriam, a blank Barbie doll who'd been left out in the sun for too long, likely had in great quantity. All around the house, women with high-end hair and designer souls were sticking their manicures beneath couch cushions and inside the slats of modernist pendant lamps. My agent, Harlan Brooks, was down there somewhere, no doubt determined to score the five back-end points Jerry was offering as the prize, and Johnny held court over a parade of models in the backyard. But I was up here, plundering Miriam Weinbach's medicine cabinet like Captain Jack Sparrow left alone on Johnny Depp's yacht.

I conjured the Sunset Boulevard Guitar Center on a Saturday afternoon. Toddlers banging on the timpani, lawyers plucking at guitars they're thinking about buying for their estranged sons, some junkie with Rod Stewart hair nodding off against a row of amps. General orderless cacophony, portending disaster. That's what the pills sounded like when they scattered across the floor: an absolute racket. And I fell with them—the high-heeled booties I was too frail to be wearing in the first place splaying out from under me, my head slamming against the fella's side of the matching his-and-her sinks. I can't be sure exactly what made me fall. Maybe I was straining to reach for a bottle of codeine buried in the back of the cabinet, or maybe I just lost the ability to stand upright. I had really taken my motor skills for granted in the years before I became enchanted by the spell of drugs: those tiny, potent assassins who, for kicks, will suddenly make your left hand incapable of following the orders your brain is trying to convey.

What I did know was that everything went dark for seconds or maybe minutes. I heard a woman shriek and then a round of clapping. The matzoh had been found. But I couldn't see anything, just a hazy imprint of the objects in the room. My phone buzzed. I raised my head from the cold tile and willed my eyes to focus as I plucked the cell from my bag. It was Johnny, and he was looking for me. *Upstrs bthrm*, I typed. *Fck.*

I lay back and watched the stars inside my head. Tried to find Orion swirling above my right eyeball. Tried to remember a point when nightfall meant something other than time to score, when the infinite sky was a reminder of the possibilities of the future and not the mistakes of the past. Back before I'd descended into my own personal hell.

"Leila?"

The door opened, and Johnny walked in. Impossible, green-eyed Johnny. Unshowered but even more handsome for it. Face of a thousand billboards. He shut the door and stared at me.

"Jesus. The hell happened to you?"

I shrugged. I felt blood trickle down my chin.

"Are you missing a tooth?"

I stuck a finger in my mouth and found a fleshy volcano.

"Christ," Johnny said. "I knew we shouldn't have gone outside today."

Johnny helped me up. He lifted me from the ground like he had so many times those last few months. But before he did, before he put his thin arms—covered in leather to hide the track marks—around my equally skinny frame, Johnny made sure to scoop up every last pill from the ground. He downed a couple and pocketed the rest for later—later that day, that week, or maybe even that hour if he was feeling ambitious.

I tried to talk, but blood gurgled in my throat. Johnny was carrying me down the steps and out the front door. He caught Harlan's eye and beckoned for my humiliated agent to follow us outside.

"Hold on. I think I'm gonna—" I managed to say just in time for Johnny to put me down so I could vomit into Jerry's pink rhododendrons. I wiped blood and puke from my mouth and sat down on the curb.

Harlan put his hand on my shoulder, then removed it as soon as he realized he'd touched a splotch of vomit. I was embarrassed, but I didn't ask him to leave. There was nothing to do but let these men take over. There was no fight left in me.

"Hey," I croaked, wiping my face on my blazer. "Johnny?"

"Yeah?" he said.

"Where was it?"

"Where was what?"

I tilted my head upward. "The matzoh?"

Johnny laughed. He wiped matted-with-upchuck hair out of my eyes. "Underneath Jerry's Oscar."

And I laughed too, a cackle that caused me to spray colored fluids from my mouth.

"Perfect," I said, and then I let Johnny and Harlan scoop me up and carry me to the car, for a ride I would come to regret sleeping through. The click of a seat belt secured my body, and I chuckled, as if external turmoil could hold a candle to the chaos raging inside my failing veins.

The sound of my own choked laughter was the last thing I remember before I regained consciousness on the floor of the East Hollywood Rehabilitation Center, weighing ninety-seven pounds at twenty-three years old, and in possession of nothing but a bloody bandage that covered my forehead, a fringe cult's satanic symbol tattooed on my hip, and a movie star's semen in my hair.

PART ONE

Just a Little Bit More

CHAPTER ONE

I was fourteen the first time I tried stimulants, alone in my bedroom with the door locked and a Sex Pistols CD playing on a loop. A brand-new *Boogie Nights* poster hung over my bed, where it covered up a constellation of glow-in-the-dark stars that, several years before, I'd applied in such a way that it outlined a very impressive accidental penis. I pulled my backpack toward me on my bed and removed a baggie containing five tiny Adderall pills, offered to me by an extremely hyperactive classmate named Tyler in exchange for letting him see his first pair of real live boobs. ("Pair" being the operative clincher here—Tyler claimed he'd already seen a single breast in a hotel peeping adventure during a family vacation.)

I hadn't asked for the drugs, but I felt a tantalizing sense of excitement the moment they were in my hands. I wasn't sure what I should do with them. I considered roping in my best friend, Mari, a tall black-haired girl who was ethnically half-devil, for a late-night adventure she undoubtedly would have been up for. Alternately, I thought about saving them for a party or a concert. But in the end, with no way of knowing exactly how I'd react and the hunch I'd want to spend some time inside my own head, I decided to be alone for the experience.

I drew the blinds over my window and switched on a lamp, trying to make my room as optimal a setting for this undertaking as possible. Satisfied with the feng shui, I slipped a little orange pill from the plastic bag and downed it with a gulp of water. After fifteen, then twenty, then twenty-one minutes, I was feeling nothing, so I did what idiotic kids have been doing since the beginning of time and will no doubt continue to do until the world is either on fire or underwater: I took another dose. Seemingly moments after I swallowed the bonus tablet, the first one hit and my heart began to race, spreading warm lightning through my veins. The first thought I had was what a good idea it was to take these pills, and the second thought I had was what a *seriously fucking good idea* it was to take these pills! The third thought I had was centered firmly around my own undeniable genius. I sang along to the music, riffing on the lyrics (sex and violence is cool, but how deep is vex and silence?), and had the idea that I ought to become a songwriter myself.

Twenty-five minutes later, the second pill kicked in, and I could feel my heartbeat in my throat. I lifted up my shirt and noticed that I could see my most vital organ pounding back and forth through a thin layer of skin. I got up to pace the room but realized movement would only make my heart beat faster. I sat back down. I hummed along with the music. I picked up a *Seventeen* magazine, an unsolicited subscription courtesy of my grandmother, and began flipping rapidly through its pages.

Just below "7 Tantalizing Tips for Spicing Up Second Base" was an ad announcing an essay contest, open to any and all teenagers residing in the fifty United States. Sponsored by D.A.R.E., the contest asked for a thousand words about why you have vowed never to do drugs. A cash prize of $300 was being offered to the winner, which, for a teenager, might as well have been a million. I read the paragraph over. Minors only, stories must be true. My confidence amped up artificially, I was certain I could write exactly the kind of essay that would win me three hundred bucks. And my speeding brain was vying to be put to use.

My heart raced, and I laughed at the delightful irony of the situa-tion. I whipped out my notebook and started jotting down ideas. What angle to take? Religion? The desire to be president one day? Juvenile renal failure? Being really into track and field? Estranged sister?

"Estranged sister" instantly felt like it would be the most fun to write. I pressed pen to paper and tried to put myself into the mind frame of a normal fourteen-year-old girl, one who would write this essay in earnest. I talked about Katrina Massey, who had been the best older sister in the world until she fell victim to the irresistible pull of narcotics. My heart beat erratically as my fingers struggled to scratch out words as quickly as I thought of them. I found myself smiling as I scribbled, my mind half-focused on the task at hand and half-attuned to the accolades that lay in my future.

It took all of thirty minutes, with a pee break included, to hammer out the essay, which I immediately typed up and printed out. I read the thing over and was rather impressed with its believability, if I did say so myself. I mailed the essay off that afternoon, finding that the most difficult part of the whole process was trying to lick a stamp with a raging case of dry mouth.

I walked back into my room, shuffled around, and decided it was time to make a collage—I needed this direly and immediately. I began to cut apart photos of models from the magazine, taking a head here, an arm there, a pair of chiseled cheekbones and a pouty lower lip. Then I glued the pieces together onto a sheet of computer paper, cre-ating a glorious composite human made of all these desirable body parts. It was totally poignant, I thought, *important*, even. Take that, Picasso! Take that, Mary Shelley! Take that, serial killers on network procedurals!

And suddenly, I was bored of collage making. So I cleaned out my sock drawer and organized the pens on my desk by color and then again by size. I did the history homework that wasn't due for a week, and then I trimmed my own hair.

After a few hours of manic thinking, I started to come down from my high. My body still felt warm and electric, but my mind wasn't as eager to complete a litany of crazy tasks. I lay down on my bed and looked up at the phallic poster that covered up the phallic constellation on my ceiling. My mind began to wander, but I didn't try to call it back. I daydreamed about my future self, watching as she drank coffee in a Paris café and paraded around a Tribeca loft—or maybe it was in Brooklyn. I saw her in London and in Los Angeles—as high up in Los Angeles as you can go—sipping drinks with her heroes, who all did spit-takes at her jokes. I watched her sit down at her computer and write page after page after brilliant page, her brain on fire, and the world eager to consume the words that flashed across her screen. And then I got a Coke from the kitchen, made myself a quesadilla, and turned on the TV.

· · ·

I ended up winning second place in the *Seventeen* contest, receiving a check for $150 and the news that my piece was going to be published in an upcoming issue of the magazine. I had completely forgotten that I'd entered the thing, so grabbing silver was more than fine with me. I used my winnings to take Mari out for a Melrose Avenue shopping spree, where we demolished piles of vintage T-shirts and snapped up the most artfully tarnished denim jackets we could find. We crammed ourselves into a single dressing room and executed a fashion show. I put on an oversized shredded shirt and posed with my hands on my hips. "Punk or bohemian?" I asked.

"Neither," Mari said. "Hippie."

"Yikes. Burn pile."

We linked arms and hopped down the street with our thrift scores stuffed into our backpacks. I felt swept up in the giddiness of a Friday afternoon, surfing a wave of pheromones that ricocheted off the teens who walked the block in throngs. "Milkshake?" I asked as we passed a Johnny Rockets.

"I have a better idea," she said, and dragged me off Melrose proper.

Local lore held that there was a homeless man named Andy who kept himself stocked in malt liquor buying cigarettes at the request of underage kids for a five-dollar fee. Mari was pretty sure she knew the alley he ran his bootlegging operation from and led us that way. The back corner of an empty parking lot had been taken over by a group of skateboarders attempting tricks off railings and trash cans. And sure enough, one of the pint-sized punks was rocking back and forth on his board while talking to a dusty bearded guy who sipped from a forty-ounce bottle of Mickey's.

Mari and I hung back at the edge of the lot and watched. "Should we just go up to him?" I asked.

"I don't know. Let's be cool for right now."

We stood for a minute, and then we moved a few feet closer. Andy's pimply partner in conversation spotted us. He leapt off his board, hitched up his pants, and strutted our way. "You ladies looking for something?"

"Yeah," Mari said. "We wanted to talk to the guy over there. Andy?"

"No one talks to Andy. You talk through me."

"Okay. We'd like a pack of Parliaments."

"I'll see what I can do," the kid said, and just stood there. "It'll cost you five bucks."

I reached into my wallet and pulled out a twenty.

"Wait," Mari said. "We should each get one."

"That'll be an extra five."

"Dude, that's kind of unreasonable."

"It's fine," I said, and nodded at the kid to take the money.

He made a big show of looking around, then slunk back over to Andy. He whispered into the Pied Piper of Tobacco's ear and handed over my bill. Andy disappeared through a hole in the chain-link fence, returning a minute later with a paper bag in each hand. He tossed the smokes to his little buddy, who brought them over to us.

"Tell him thanks," I said. The kid just nodded and puffed out his chest.

Mari opened one of the packs and pulled out a pair of cigarettes. We bummed a light off an enthusiastically cologned man outside a sneaker shop and hunched over, on the lookout for bored cops. Then we made our way back to Mari's house to get ready for a night that was to include real proximity to her brother, Devon—dreamy Devon, that glorious postpubescent specimen whose name had been doodled in the margins of every notebook I'd owned since middle school.

Devon's band was playing a birthday party in Encino, and I'd convinced Mari it was her sisterly duty to attend, best friend in tow, of course. We slid into the tightest selections from our new wardrobes, straightened our hair, and eyelinered cat eyes above our lashes. *Not bad, Massey,* I thought, looking myself over in Mari's full-length mirror. I looked mature, grown-up, *at least* fifteen.

Mari and I bounded down the steps and into the kitchen, where Devon and his bandmates hovered by the table, passing around a joint. The boys turned their heads when we walked in. The spikiest of them, a guy named Keefo, looked Mari up and down and made a jerk-off motion with his hand. Mari punched him in the arm, but the corners of her lips betrayed her.

"You guys look cool," Devon said, smiling at me and sending my heart soaring into my esophagus. The joint reached him, and he took a hit, closing his eyes as he sucked in the smoke.

He turned to me, looking dazed. "Leila, you want some?"

I hesitated.

"You don't have to."

"Um."

"Leila's, like, a genius," Devon said to his pals, who wore their standard uniform of safety-pin earrings and ripped-up plaid pants. "She got, like, this special certificate from the government last year? For, like, being so good at school? I don't know why she hangs out with my retard sister."

Mari stuck her tongue out at Devon, flashing a metal piercing. Although it thrilled me to learn that Devon knew *actual facts* about me, I wanted him to stop sharing them before a calculator and a pocket protector replaced my body in the eyes of all those guys. So I took the joint from Devon's hand and inhaled, mimicking what I'd seen the rest of the table do and trying with every muscle in my body to avoid coughing. It almost worked.

"Damn," one of the guys said. "We shouldn't've smoked all that weed. Now we're gonna be too tired to play the show."

"You're right," Devon said. "Check the fridge for Red Bull."

When no Red Bull was found, I experienced a moment of pure internal conflict—perhaps the most ambivalent feeling I'd encountered in my young life so far. I had what was left of my second round of Tyler pills (he actually got to touch a boob this time) right there in my bag. I could share them with Devon and his friends, solving their problem and making me the hero of the evening. But then, of course, I wouldn't have the drugs anymore.

"I, um, I've got something that might help," I was saying before I'd even made the conscious decision to loose the words.

All the boys and even Mari looked me over curiously. I pulled out the baggie and withdrew two of the remaining pills. "It's Adderall. We could probably, like, chop it up or something."

"Dope," Keefo said, and immediately got to work crushing and refining the pills with his school ID. He rolled a dollar and snorted a line, then passed the bill around the table. The powder went up my nose with surprising ease, burning just a little. It hit quickly. *Well, holy shit.* My heart raced, and I began talking like an auctioneer, asking Devon and his friends what time their band was going on and if we could get a ride, and God, doesn't this just feel so fucking good?

Devon laughed at me a few times, in a good-natured way that only made me feel more amazing. At the birthday party in Encino that night, Mari and I kept taking trips to the bathroom to snort up the last bits of Adderall, somehow always finding more microscopic specks of orange powder at the bottom of the baggie. Then we'd head outside, yank cigarettes from our packs, and smoke them down to the filter. My throat was ravaged, but I didn't care. We danced up front while the band played, and elbowed anyone who got in our way. By the time we found ourselves back at Mari's, my skin was crawling and I felt like I hadn't showered since toddlerhood. I was gross in a way that seemed very adult. Mari and I stumbled into her bed, where we stayed up until dawn recapping the events of the night, finally feeling like we were the kind of girls who fit in at parties. She told me she'd never seen me look so cool as when I was pushing through those throngs of kids, knowing exactly where I wanted to be and refusing to let anyone stop me from getting there. I told her she looked hot in her new clothes, and we both agreed that Keefo had a giant crush on her. I vowed to get us more Adderall, pronto.

．　．　．

The first time I did drugs, I felt brilliant. The second time, I saw my overly conscious self disappear as it was conquered by an influx of chemical confidence. The third time I did drugs bled right into the fourth time, and that was how I became a teenage addict.

Chapter Two

It's been said that addiction runs in the family, that the desire to chemically alter ourselves burrows its way into our DNA and lies in patient wait until we've already embraced it without realizing it had been there all along. This was certainly true of my own family, although I had to stumble on that fact incidentally—because pretending, and even straight-up lying, is a part of my genetics too. We were one of those everything-is-going-to-be-just-fine clans, capable of ignoring problems, of shifting our vision to frame out red flags.

My mother was a two-glasses-of-wine-at-dinner drinker, nothing immoderate or obscene, always just enough to take the edge off. And my father never drank at all, not a beer after work or a glass of scotch before bed. My dad's abstention wasn't discussed or made an example of; it was simply an accepted fact of dinnertime, like how my mom was going to tell a story about someone behaving rudely in the grocery store or say that the chicken was dry.

My dad was a quiet man, well-spoken and sometimes stunningly clever, but never looking to be the center of attention. He worked in advertising, writing concise copy about the sleekness of a convertible or the potency of an energy drink. He made a comfortable enough living and never talked much about his work one way or the other. When he had time off, he concerned himself mostly with Dodgers baseball and heavy historical fiction.

I looked up to my father, although I never felt like I *knew* him. He was present and attentive, by all measurable standards a good parent, but I often wondered about his interior life, suspecting it might be much more interesting than his day-to-day facade of office work and televised baseball games. I got the sense he had stumbled into an existence of clever slogans and pleasant-enough domesticity, and never quite felt like he was alive inside of it.

It wasn't until I was twelve that the way I thought about my dad changed—or, rather, it started to fall into place. I was wandering the garage in search of a glue gun and construction paper so I could make my science fair project as aesthetically pleasing as possible to compensate for my lousy methodology. (I still haven't lost belief in the idea that a little glitter can cover up some pretty big mistakes—same goes for practiced cursive and eyeliner.) I found a crate full of childhood art supplies, which I sifted through, pulling out anything colorful or shiny. I tossed aside spin-art kits and finger paint until all that was left was an unlabeled box at the bottom of the crate. It was rubber-banded shut several times over, clearly intended to stay hidden in a place no one was likely to look.

The rubber bands crumbled as soon as I touched them. I lifted the box's dusty lid, hoping I wasn't about to stumble upon a secret stash of pornography or something even more upsetting, like a stack of self-help books. Instead, I pulled out a yellowed manuscript, three hundred typewritten pages, with my dad's name on the author line. A second copy sat beneath, covered in faded chicken-scratch. I flipped through the first few pages, then sat down on the floor to read the thing in earnest.

It was a thinly veiled roman à clef, with a narrator characterized as "dark in the eyes but bright throughout the rest of the face, just angular enough to be handsome instead of threatening," a physical description so accurate to my father that it stunned me he was able to capture it. The book started with a chapter about the narrator's childhood in Baltimore, and then leapt to his high-school years, where he was a late addition to the bandwagon against the Vietnam War. He took weekend trips into New York City to protest, and wandered around the East Village with liberated college girls who found his innocence adorable. Some of the words were faded, and page twenty-eight ripped when I turned it too speedily, but the book felt alive in my hands.

"Leila," I heard my mother call from the kitchen. "Can you come set the table?"

I quickly dropped the manuscript and hid the box. Downstairs, my mom asked how my project was coming, and I lied and said it actually wasn't due for another week, knowing there was no way I would finish it in time, not now that I had something much more interesting to concentrate on. During the meal, I couldn't stop watching my father eat his spaghetti and meatballs; even the way he held his fork was now loaded with subtext. He ate delicately, twirling the pasta through the prongs like he might have done with a flower child's hair during a mild spring day on Saint Marks Place.

The next morning, I faked a cold so I could stay home from school, and I snuck back into the garage once my parents left for work. I picked up right as my father started experimenting with marijuana and psychedelics, which led to a blur of hazy years. There were nights of existential debates inside coffee shops, a long and winding road trip out West, and a story about robbing a Wendy's with a samurai sword, demanding ten hamburgers or the little redhead gets it. My father's character was adventurous and wise beyond his years. He was the one who sat shotgun with the hitchhiker-friendly trucker while his friends all got high in the backseat and nodded off; he and the trucker talked road philosophy (while getting high in the front seat) all across the expanse of America.

But as the story went on, my father's character became more and more dependent on the drugs that had started out as a tool for expansion and escape. The psychedelics had made him paranoid, and he was relying on downers to get through his days without panic attacks. The last chapter of the book revealed a drug-fueled psychotic break and a trip to a mental institution, where a diet of Thorazine and bland TV eventually restored him to sanity.

There were so many character details that rang true about my father that I couldn't help but read the book as wholly autobiographical, and at the end of it I felt like I sort of understood my dad. I felt close to him. I also heard echoes of myself in some of the descriptions—and some part of me decided right then and there that I was predisposed to live out an addiction narrative of my own.

I wondered how much of this story my mother knew. She wasn't a prude, exactly, but I got the sense she'd never experimented. My mom seemed okay with the unexamined life, finding the trajectory of completing daily tasks satisfying enough. She worked as an administrator in the LA public-school system, at first with the goal of making a difference, but then only with aspirations of not screwing anything up too badly. She clocked in and out, then came home, where she enjoyed cooking hearty meals she could then reconstitute a second time around (beef stew on Wednesday filled a potpie on Friday). She was in a book club where no one ever finished the material but where everyone talked long into the night anyway. She always seemed happy enough.

But I was pretending just as much as they were, and hiding things I knew my mom and dad wouldn't want to deal with. It was a habit that started young. I never asked the same questions other little kids did. Of course Santa Claus wasn't real—the timeline was impractical, and a man that obese would have died of diabetes long ago. But I found it fascinating that, in a universe where so much of daily life was all about keeping strangers from penetrating the bubble, the ultimate childhood hero was a guy who popped down through the chimney bearing Tonka trucks and Easy-Bake Ovens, and left immediately, asking for nothing in return. I didn't want to know if Santa was real; I wanted to know if there were actually people like that—selfless individuals who genuinely cared about the happiness of others above all else—and if our mantra of "stranger danger" wasn't limiting exposure to those folks. What my parents extrapolated from my inquiries was that I was aching to get to know some overly friendly foreign adults, and that freaked them out completely. So I shut up about Santa Claus and stopped asking those kinds of questions anywhere outside the confines of my own head. I became one thing on the surface and something entirely different inside. But the persona I was crafting for myself was still a work in progress, and I didn't always lie as well as I thought I did.

I had been coming down the stairs for a glass of juice the day I heard my parents fighting about me. I was ten, and the juice I was after was my own cocktail of lemonade and unsweetened cranberry, which I liked to rub across my lips until they turned bright red. I paused on the top step when I heard the word "cut" come out of my mother's mouth. I rolled up the sleeve of my T-shirt and looked at my left arm, just below the shoulder, where two deep slashes ran parallel to one another. The cuts had been my way of coping with getting disinvited to a sleepover by the new girl in my friend group. They still stung, but only when I remembered they were there.

"She said she scraped herself climbing a tree," my mother told my father.

"And you don't believe her?"

"They don't look like the kind of cuts you get from climbing a tree."

My dad sighed long and hard. "Beth, she's ten years old."

"Which is exactly why I'm so concerned. She's supposed to be a carefree little girl, not some morbid creature who stays up late writing in notebooks and staring out the window. When's the last time you saw her climb a tree?"

"I've seen her climb trees," my father said.

"Have you really?"

The helpless silence that issued from my father's mouth made it hard for me to breathe. I hated the way I felt, and I hated the way he felt. I dug my nails into the flesh of my palm until tiny droplets of blood appeared on the surface.

I turned around and headed back toward my room, making a silent vow to become better at hiding my thoughts from the outside world. I pledged to start climbing trees. I heard the front door close and the sound of my father's footsteps on concrete. My heart still stung a little back then, but only when I remembered it was there.

CHAPTER THREE

Yes, there was some melancholy to my childhood, but it wasn't all ruminations on self-harm and the morality of the Easter Bunny. I also had fun, like when I was careening through the loop of a roller coaster at a hundred miles per hour with a scream suspended in my throat, or the first time I got really drunk, off vodka and orange juice, with Mari.

Mari and Devon's mother, Diane, was a dental hygienist whose only rule of parenting was that there was no sugar allowed in the house. Diane had a fraught relationship with her second husband, Tony, and often took off for days at a time to either track him down or, once he'd been found, rekindle the spark in romantic Las Vegas.

I knew Diane was on one of those trips the day Mari showed up to eighth-grade English with a blue-raspberry tongue, trailing a chemical cloud of her mother's perfume. I cornered her by her locker.

"I'm sleeping over tonight," I said. "Give me something to tell my parents."

"Study night? For the Jack London exam?"

"We took that test last week."

"Did we?" Mari winced. "Oops."

Mari's house screamed "parents out of town" at the top of its lungs from the moment we walked in. Dishes were piled high in the sink; last night's chosen TV channel still blared. On the counter was a dwindling stack of twenties and the pile of pizza boxes the money had gone toward. There was also a mostly full bottle of Smirnoff with the cap off. Mari said that she and Devon had each had a glass the day before, but tonight we were going to get fucked-up.

"It doesn't even taste that nasty if you hold your nose," she said when she saw the grimace on my face. "Or we could just do shots. That's how Devon rolls. He'll be here later."

That was all I needed to hear. Ever since the night we'd gone to see his band play, I'd become convinced it was only a matter of time before Devon and I fell passionately into one another's arms. In my head, I played out the rest of the evening. Devon would open the front door, spot me on the couch with my legs folded and a cocktail in my hand, and there would be a moment where he physically wouldn't be able to pull his eyes away from me. In this vision, I was wearing velvet and had developed the throaty purr of Katharine Hepburn.

"Oh, hello, Devon," I'd say. "We're just having some alcoholic beverages. Won't you join me on . . . oh, what is this called . . . the love seat?"

In reality, what happened was that Mari poured us each a glass of vodka with a heavy helping of OJ, and I was woozy and giggling after three sips. Devon did soon swoosh through the front door, but right behind him was a girl in a tight tank top and dyed-red hair. She chewed gum in a way that felt like a series of accusations, and no one in the room bore any resemblance whatsoever to a Hepburn. My fantasy vanished at the sight of this girl, and I couldn't even look at Devon as he threw down his backpack and made a beeline for the bottle of Smirnoff.

"Wheeeeeere are you taking that?" Mari asked, swaying a little.

"Me and Kristin are gonna go upstairs. Tell us when pizza's here."

"You better not steal it all. Leila and I are getting drunk tonight."

Devon's eyes darted to the couch, where I was staring with great interest at a melting ice cube in my glass. I looked up from my drink, he nodded at me, and I smiled widely. He laughed a little and turned back to his girl and her smacking Trident. "Whatever. There's another bottle in the pantry."

I was quiet for a minute as I replayed Devon's laugh in my head. I downed the rest of my drink and hobbled over to the counter for more.

"Oh my God," she said. "You're so mad. Are you, like, in love with my brother or something?"

"No. Shut up. I'm just drunk."

"I wonder if he's gonna do it with that girl. He has before, you know."

"You're lying. Devon has had sex?"

"Uh-huh. My stepdad's niece stayed with us for a little bit, because her mom had some sort of breakdown. And she, like, zoned in on my brother and straight-up stole his virginity. You're prettier than her, though, so don't worry."

"I'm not worried. I don't even care."

"You're just such a prude, though. How many guys have you even kissed—like three?"

"Yeah." The answer was two.

"Lemme see your technique." Mari plopped down next to me on the couch and turned her face toward mine. I giggled but didn't protest when she leaned forward and stuck her tongue in my mouth. After a few seconds, she pulled away.

"Not bad, but you need to slow down. Relax."

She kissed me again and swirled her tongue around in my mouth. I concentrated on slowing myself down, letting the alcohol in my body dictate a rhythm. Mari bit my lip with her front teeth, and then I did the same back to her.

"Okay, that was pretty dope," she said, leaning back onto the couch. "Do the lip thing. Guys love that, because they never expect it."

I nodded, ready for another lesson, but Mari was done. She turned on the TV and ordered a pizza. We watched shitty reality shows, clapping whenever a hot guy came on the screen and yelling "That's your boyfriend!" when an unfortunate-looking one appeared. We were both asleep by 10 p.m., drunk baby lambs surrounded by empty glasses and dropped pieces of pepperoni.

The next morning was a catastrophe of pounding headaches and dry mouth. Mari and I downed Advil and swished mouthwash before we ran out the door, already late. But it didn't matter how hungover I felt—there was a spring in my step and a secret smile on my lips all day. I was a good kisser now, and someone who knew what it felt like to be intoxicated.

I went up to Mari at lunch with an extra can of Diet Coke, and we sat down on the grass. "Okay, I think I'm still drunk," I said.

"Yeah, me too. Makes History kind of tolerable, at least."

I nodded. We both felt *so over it* as we watched all the normal, boring, sober people do all their normal, boring, sober lunchtime activities.

"Hey," I said, pointing to a guy who was walking swiftly toward the main building. "I bet he would like the lip thing."

Mari's mouth dropped open, and she smacked me on the arm, delighted. It was our English teacher, Mr. Shelling, and neither of us would ever get through his class again without looking at each other, biting down on our lips, and cracking up.

FANTASY SEQUENCE:

INT. MARI'S HOUSE — DAY

The room is a mess, with pizza boxes strewn everywhere.
LEILA (14, think a young Katharine Hepburn) sits
on the couch in a velvet camisole. She sips from a
screwdriver.

Across the room, MARI (14, think a young Veronica Lake)
mixes herself a drink.

                    MARI
          We could do some shots. That's what
          my brother does. He'll be here
          soon.

                    LEILA
          Cool. Whatever. I'm up for
          anything.

The door swings open. DEVON (15, think a young James
Dean, or actually, just James Dean) walks in. Behind
him is GUM GIRL (15, think a young hippopotamus).

                    MARI
          Hey, bro. We were just about to do
          some shots.

                    DEVON
          Who's we? Oh--

Devon swivels his head and catches sight of Leila on
the couch. He's speechless for a moment, but he quickly
pulls it together.

> DEVON
>
> Great. I could be up for shots.

> GUM GIRL
>
> Um, I thought you wanted to play me
> that record.

> DEVON
>
> Yeah. The Velvet Underground and
> Nico. It's my favorite.

> LEILA
> (in a throaty purr)
> No way. That's my favorite record
> too.

> DEVON
>
> Are you serious? It's got some of
> the best songs ever, right?

> LEILA
>
> Totally. And I just love Nico's
> voice.

> DEVON
>
> You know what? You kind of sound
> like Nico. Seriously. Sort of a
> throaty purr.

Leila laughs. Takes a sip of her screwdriver. Gum girl
chews angrily.

                         MARI
              Okay, dweebs. Let's do shots and
              then we can all go listen to it.

Mari pours the vodka out into four glasses. Devon and
Leila look at each other, and they both smile.

Chapter Four

My amphetamine habit was a fully formed organism by the time I entered my junior year of high school. It was my main indulgence, and substances like booze and pot were simply things I consumed on weekends to keep up appearances. I pledged daily allegiance to Adderall, thanking the heavens above for inventing this legal kiddy-speed that came in beautiful discs of bright-orange and blue.

A steady supply of pills was shockingly easy to come by—half the kids I went to school with had been diagnosed with ADHD, and they'd sell off their leftovers at the end of the month. I considered faking a concentration problem and scoring a prescription of my own, but that would have involved bringing my parents into things, and I figured out early on that keeping my folks in the dark about every aspect of my life was the best way to ensure I could do whatever I wanted.

I subsidized my habit by stealing my own lunch money. The drug took my appetite right out from under me—a fine problem for a budding teenage girl to have—so I'd forgo sloppy joes from the cafeteria and hand over the cash my folks doled out, receiving a pile of twenty-milligram tablets in exchange. Within months, I was scarfing one pill in the morning to get through the school day, another in the afternoon to bang out my homework, and one more in the evening, just because I'd earned it. School became a breeze for me—my very good academic record soon became spectacular, which made it very easy for me to rationalize my pill consumption. There was no reason to stop, because everything was going so well. Sure, I was lying and stealing to keep my habit subsidized, but such a marvelous and inquisitive student as myself couldn't possibly have a problem.

The first time I understood that I was an addict, through and through, was the first time I tried to go three days without drugs. I was somewhere around fifty hours sans stimulants when I became convinced my head was actually about to explode, splattering a mixture of Civil War dates and algebra equations and Bob Dylan lyrics onto the wall.

"Leila, did you get the difference between diffusion and osmosis?" A high voice penetrated my skull and echoed back and forth inside my brain. "Something about, like, a membrane barrier?"

It took a minute before I could make sense of the words, but at least I was pretty sure the voice belonged to Chessa. Yes, Chessa was her name, and we were in her bedroom, sitting on overstuffed pink bean-bag chairs, surrounded by dozens of ceramic ducks. I forced myself to focus, first zooming in on the venti coffee cup in my hand and then absorbing the nervous look on Chessa's freckled face. I had the sudden urge to play connect-the-dots across her skin, and was pretty sure I could even find a duck.

"Leila?" Chessa flipped a page in the biology textbook that sat in her lap, and that's when things clicked into place. Chessa was my lab partner, and we were inside her cotton-candy bedroom working on our cell membrane project.

"The difference. Right," I said. "I think it has to do with, like, the angle of refraction. No, wait, that's a physics word."

"Hey, are you okay?" Chessa asked. "I mean, you look kind of sick."

"Can I use your bathroom?"

"For sure," Chessa said, and pointed to the door at the end of a periwinkle hall.

Inside the Glade-fresh bathroom, I gulped down the rest of my coffee and tossed the cup into the trash. I looked in the mirror and examined the pair of dark circles that had begun to spread aggressively outward from beneath my eyes like they were determined to claim my entire face, turning me into a human bruise. Holy shit, did I feel like death.

With the Grim Reaper hacking at my bones and breathing through my pores, I officially regretted the decision to give my body a break from drugs. My organs felt like barbells, and my brain, a bowl of lukewarm oatmeal. I sat down on the toilet to pee.

"Leila? Leila? Oh my God, are you okay?" It was Chessa's shrill, electrified voice again, but it came to me through a barrier of fog. "I thought you might be . . . like, dead."

Chessa was standing over me. I focused on her round face and her plaid headband. I started to count freckles.

"I'm so sorry," she said. "When you didn't come back, I called your name for a while and then I knocked. But you weren't answering, so I came in."

The words washed over me as I grasped at pieces of my brain and tried to organize them into something resembling a concrete thought. Seventeen freckles on her left cheek. Three on the tip of her nose. A sparkling-clean bathroom, the smell of chemical flowers, and me, with my pants down around my ankles. Because I'd fallen asleep on my lab partner's toilet in the middle of the afternoon.

"It's okay," I said to Chessa, who appeared very much like she was about to cry. "I'm just gonna, you know, finish up."

Chessa left the room. I flushed the toilet and washed my hands and face, letting the cool water diffuse and osmosis into my toxic pores.

"Well, that was weird," I said, walking back into Chessa's bedroom. "I guess I must be coming down with something."

Chessa handed me a glass of ice water, still appearing quite ter-rified. "The flu's totally going around," she said, "so maybe it's that?"

I nodded, and she pointed to her fluffy pink bed. The sheets were patterned with cartoon ducks. "Do you want to take a nap or something?"

I climbed into Chessa's bed without even answering, managing to kick off my boots but still wearing a pair of stiff denim pants and a jacket. I fell back to sleep instantly, a deep, dreamless black hole that felt like a magnet wiping out my internal hard drive.

When I woke up hours later, it was dark outside, and Chessa and her mother were standing over me. Chessa's mom held out a bowl of chicken noodle soup. "You poor thing," the mother said in a voice even higher than her daughter's. "We thought you might want some dinner."

I inhaled a whiff of soup, and something grabbed me from the inside of my stomach. It squeezed and squeezed, and I panicked until I realized: *This is hunger. This is what it feels like to be hungry.* I took the soup and drained it like I was a wild animal annihilating a fresh kill. "Uh, thanks," I said.

Chessa's mom put her hand up to my head. "You feel warm, sweet-heart. It's that darn flu, I bet."

"Leila, you can totally sleep over if you want," Chessa said. "Should I call your parents or something?"

"It's okay. I'll text them," I said. I started to type out a message but fell asleep before I pressed "Send."

In the morning, I felt rested. I checked my phone, and there were ten missed calls from home. I climbed out of bed and headed for the bathroom, where I ran into Chessa exiting another room in her paja-mas. "Hey, you're up," she said. "How do you feel?"

"A little better, I think." My jacket clung to me, and I must have smelled like roadkill. I wondered if my parents had called the cops, like they did the last time I just forgot to go home. "I guess I should go shower and change before school."

"Yeah, cool. Well, I'll see you in class."

"Shit." I suddenly remembered. "What about our bio project?"

"Oh, don't worry about it," Chessa said, tugging at her flannel ducks. "I finished it last night. And I called your mom, just in case. She says hi."

CHAPTER FIVE

Instead of looking at the night with Chessa as a cautionary tale, I came away from the experience fully convinced that it was absolutely necessary to my academic survival for me to be on Adderall all the time. So I redoubled my efforts to make sure that I was high pretty much constantly, which became even easier after I met Griffin—my pseudo-boyfriend for most of junior year, the taker of my virginity, and, most importantly, my introduction to cocaine.

He was a private-school senior with a pair of wily blue eyes, who lived in a huge glassy house in Laurel Canyon, the prize jewel of Los Angeles. The neighborhood is a haven of amber sunshine that melts slowly over the hills, fossilizing the palm trees and million-dollar homes. Sometimes a wind will disrupt the stillness, or a hawk or a Porsche 911, but for the most part it truly is beautiful and serene. What goes on inside those houses is another story altogether.

I practically lived at Griffin's house during my spring break, drinking lemonade, ashing cigarettes into the infinity pool, and turning down the music whenever Grif's parents called to check in from the Maldives. One day, he invited some of his private-school buddies over for a barbecue. I walked inside and heard him on the phone, placing an order. "A pack of hamburger buns, a thing of blue cheese. Throw in an onion. And two six-packs of Modelo."

I shot him a look at the mention of beer.

He smiled. "Thanks a lot," he said. "And see you soon."

"Two questions," I said. "*Uno*: did you just order beer? And *dos*: do you actually expect that to work?"

"Oh yeah, it'll work. I've been doing this since I was twelve. Dude at the store isn't going to drive all the way up here, on these crazy-ass roads, just to bail once he sees I'm underage. Especially if I toss him a nice tip."

He was completely right, and pretty soon I was floating in the pool with a beer in one hand and a cigarette in the other. When I heard Griffin's friends drive up, I hopped out, throwing a threadbare Lou Reed T-shirt on over my red bikini top. One of the kids was a Disney Channel heartthrob named Jasper, who pretended to be an orphaned rock star for preteen girls every Monday at 5 p.m. If spiral notebooks and pencil pouches bearing one's image were a sign a person has made it, then Jasper was a bona fide Hollywood legend. In tow was Jasper's girlfriend, Jessika, who wore knee-high boots over studded jeans and was a good five years older than her beau.

Jasper ditched more beer and a bottle of champagne on the table. A scrappy half-goateed guy named Toby slimed up behind them, hands thrust deep into the pockets of his baggy jeans.

"I'm so hungry I could eat, like, a meal!" Jessika yelled, bouncing up and down.

Grif came out with a plate of caprese and set it on the table. He jerked his head in my direction, and I folded my legs under me. "Guys, this is Leila."

"Oh my God, she's a *baby*!" Jessika sat down behind me and began braiding my hair. She took the cigarette from my mouth and placed it in her own. "Griffin, she's adorable."

I made eye contact with Griffin, and he winked, something I'd seen him practice in front of the mirror like a proper future grown-up asshole. Jasper popped open the bottle of champagne and gulped straight from the lip. "Gift from a Disney exec," he explained before passing it around.

We ate our hamburgers with arugula, and Griffin's friends told stories about him—like the time he took his dad's Emmy in for show-and-tell and lost it (his pop never noticed) and the time he hit a baseball through the window of Michael Bay's Hummer (he was grounded for a week). After dinner, we stayed at the table finishing the beer. Toby was curating a playlist on Griffin's laptop and complaining about the lack of quality hip-hop. Jasper cleared his throat and nodded to Jessika.

"Yo, Grif," Jasper said. "You got a mirror or a platter or something?"

"Uh, probably. What for?"

"Or just, like, something flat and clean?"

My heart leapt, because I knew what was coming.

"I'll get it." Jessika walked into the house and returned with a silver serving tray. She set it on the table and pulled a small bag of powder from her purse.

"Wait," Griffin said. "Is that—?"

"It's cocaine, you twat." Jasper snickered.

"Gift from Mickey Mouse?" I asked, and everyone laughed.

Jasper pulled out his SAG card and cut lines. When the platter was passed to me, I leaned over and snorted the coke in one deft inhalation. The truth was, although my bloodstream had not yet experienced the anarchic flurry of a line of cocaine, I had already become something of an expert at chopping up my Adderall and siphoning the orange powder. It had become my preferred method of ingestion, much to the chagrin of my delicate nasal cavities.

But this stuff was different. Stronger, of course, but also somehow lighter and more joyful. I felt immediately like I was a goddamn god, if we're being perfectly honest. I was Kate Moss and Tiny Fey all at once, and, well, I *fucking so totally loved* these friends of Griffin's. With all my shaky little heart.

We stayed out there snorting for what must have been hours, but felt like seconds and centuries all at once. At some point, one of us wanted more booze, so we all piled into Jasper's Escalade and went soaring down Mulholland. I was sitting on Griffin's lap, and I stuck my head out the window to watch the city glitter aggressively down below.

"This feels good," I whispered into Griffin's ear. He put his hand on my neck and turned my face into his.

Toby got a sudden craving for a milkshake, so we ended up in a back booth at Mel's Drive-In. I was still wearing that Lou Reed T-shirt over a bikini, but at least I'd managed to slip my boots on before we'd left Griffin's house. It was 2 a.m., and a pair of tweakers sat in the corner. They both had fluorescent-yellow hair spiked high above their heads. They kept looking over at our table. Finally, one of them turned to Jasper and said, "Hey. Aren't you the Gavin? From *Davin, Gavin, and Avin*?"

Jasper shrugged.

"Dude, you totally are!"

Jessika snickered and asked, "You watch the Disney Channel?"

"Man, I watch everything. You ever catch those ShamWow infomercials late at night? With that psychotic Israeli dude?"

Jessika shook her head.

"The pathos of that motherfucker is goddamned palpable."

"Amen," I replied, and we all nodded stoically.

Our waitress came over, interrupting the tweaker's oral dissertation on the reusable-paper-towel advertising industry. Toby ordered three milkshakes—chocolate, vanilla, and strawberry—just for himself, yet somehow it was me the waitress glared at while she jotted down her shorthand.

When she left, Griffin handed me a napkin. "Leila, your fucking nose is bleeding like crazy."

"Oh shit." There was, in fact, blood everywhere. Down my face, and all over Lou Reed's too. "Weird, I didn't notice."

"You can't feel that?" Griffin asked, more accusatorily than seemed fair.

"Come on." Jessika leapt up and steered me by the arm into the bathroom. She kept handing me paper towels while I washed myself off. When the bleeding stopped, she pulled makeup from her bag and painted my face.

"There. Now you look like a movie star."

I moved to wipe a last bit of blood from my nose, but Jessika stopped me. "Leave it. More authentic that way."

I smiled. "Someone call the paparazzi."

Jessika pulled what was left of the cocaine from her purse. "You really like this stuff, huh?"

"Uh, I guess," I stammered. *Is it that obvious?* "I mean, like, it's fun."

"Want a little more?"

"Sure. Why not? But only if you are."

Jessika did a bump off her car key, black with a Mercedes logo, and made one for me.

"Other nostril, sweetie."

I snorted the molehill and then one more. Somehow, I was even higher than before. I could feel the bright colors of the diner in my bloodstream, and the '60s tunes coming from the jukebox in the follicles of my hair. Jessika and I went outside to smoke. One of the tweakers was there too, sucking at a Marlboro like it was an asthma inhaler. He looked at me and Jessika standing there high as kites in our heavy makeup, she in her studs and me without pants. "Hey," he rasped. "I'll pay you chicks a hundred bucks to make out."

And we did. Jessika and I swapped spit right there in the Mel's parking lot. But the guy didn't have a hundred bucks.

CHAPTER SIX

Bored with schoolwork that had become entirely too easy, I decided that junior year was as good a time as any to embrace what I thought of as my destiny—so I launched my career as a professional writer. Fueled by a constant stream of synthetic energy, I began scribbling plays, biting little slices of American teenage life. My favorite of these one-acts can be described as an updated *Breakfast Club* set at a rave. A group of kids from different social strata find themselves huddled in the corner of a dusty warehouse, rolling on ecstasy and petting at one another's hair. Under the magical sway of the lovey-dovey drug, they solve all the problems of high-school politics—only to forget everything they'd figured out come morning. The play included lines of dialogue like:

```
                   KEVIN
      So if hell is other people, that
      means heaven's just yourself? That
      doesn't sound so great either.
```

I used the thing for an eleventh-grade English class assignment, and sensitive old Mr. Consuelo liked it so much he had me work with the drama department to stage a little reading. He invited the owner of a local joint called the Last Theater, a gaunt and wild-eyed fellow named Ron, who decided to produce the thing for real as part of his spring showcase. So there I was, just sixteen and with my name on a real live Los Angeles marquee. Well, almost my name—the theater was missing a couple of signage letters, so for a period of time I became known as L3ILA MASS3Y.

My ecstasy one-act did pretty well thanks to a little write-up in the *LA Times* calling me "like a teenage Arthur Miller," and Ron commissioned me to write something else—a longer play in the same vein as the first one. It didn't take me long to settle on a topic. They say you should write what you know, and what I knew at this point in my life better than just about anything else was Adderall. So I set about crafting a simple love story between two teenagers who get high on uppers and go through all the stages of a relationship in a single night. It featured lines like:

> STEPHANIE
> Parting is such sweet sorrow
> that, fuck it, let's stay up eat-
> ing Doritos in bed until our
> tongues are bloody and we can't see
> straight. Deal?

I was feeling totally on edge the day the play was set to open, so I compensated by taking even more pills than usual—which, of course, only further amped my nerves and turned the butterflies in my stomach into various incarnations of Mothra. I found myself pacing the halls right before showtime, reciting dialogue from the play even though there was absolutely no need for me to have it memorized. I could hear murmuring from inside the theater as people settled into their seats. I figured it was time to get my shit together and head inside, but before I could, the door swung open and Ron dashed out. He placed his hand on my shoulder.

"Hey," he said. "I've been looking for you. We've got a full house in there."

"That's awesome."

"I want to introduce you before the curtain goes up."

"Cool. Am I supposed to say something, or—?"

"If you want to, absolutely."

I felt sweaty and wondered if it showed. I took a deep breath and smoothed my hair. Ron rushed me inside, and we walked onto the stage. He thanked the audience for coming, offered some kind words about his staff, and introduced me with a peppering of accolades like "brilliant," "wise beyond her years," and even "the voice of a generation." I was only able to take in half of what he said, more focused on the blood rushing my brain and how my body felt like doing jumping jacks so that it wouldn't explode.

The audience applauded, and then there was silence. They were waiting for me to speak, but all I could do was stare at the crowd, eyes roaming across middle-agers, college theater types, and even a couple of kids from my school. There was a monologue in my head, but I couldn't latch on to it. I knew I should talk a little about how the play came to be. And I should thank Ron and Mr. Consuelo. But I couldn't figure out which I needed to do first.

I got the idea to imagine the crowd in their underwear, but I immediately got too invested in getting the characters right. Hanes or Calvins on the pretty gay boy with the pouty lips? And the purple-haired woman in the front row screamed "granny panties," but perhaps she played against type and wore a thong under her flowing skirt?

They all stared at me, just waiting, until I was finally able to open my mouth.

"Hi."

No one said it back.

"I'm Leila."

They already knew that, didn't they?

"You know what? I think I'm really nervous."

A few people smiled sympathetically, including Purple Hair—which definitely seemed like a granny-panty move.

"Anyway, I hope you like the play. And if you don't, well, I hope you're a good liar."

I got a few laughs, but it didn't stop my face from flushing shades of raspberry sherbet. If there had been a whip around, I would have flogged myself right there on the stage. I was so high I couldn't think straight, and I needed something to calm me down.

I walked behind the curtain and left the theater through the backstage exit. Earlier, I had helped Ron set up the building's spare room for an after-party, and I headed straight there. There were bottles of cheap liquor on the table next to packages of cookies, and a little disco ball hung from the ceiling.

I was alone in the room, which suddenly felt piercingly bright. My heart raced, and my mouth tasted bitter. I turned off the lights. I swiped a bottle of whiskey and sat down on the floor beneath a folding table.

"I think I'm nervous?" I said aloud to no one. "Very professional, genius."

I opened the whiskey and sipped straight from the bottle, trying to drink away my exploding nerves and forget the night before it had even ended.

INT. AFTER-PARTY ROOM — NIGHT

Roughly two dozen people are in the room, talking and
drinking. The disco light spins above.

The door opens, and Leila walks in. She's a little wobbly and clearly drunk. She surveys the room but hangs
back.

Ron spots her and darts over. He throws his arms around
her in a giant hug.

                         RON
          Congratulations!

                        LEILA
          Oh. Um, thanks.

                         RON
          So, what did you think?

Leila scrunches up her face guiltily.

                         RON
          You . . . didn't watch, did you?

                        LEILA
          I couldn't. I don't know why I got
          so freaked-out.

She looks down.

                    RON
Well, you'll catch the next one.
People loved it, kiddo. We're a
hit.

                    LEILA
Seriously?

                    RON
Don't sound so surprised.

A COLLEGE-AGED GUY standing behind them turns around.

                    GUY
Okay, I probably shouldn't say anything, but I was sitting next to
the reviewer from the Weekly. And I
got a look at his notes.

                    LEILA
Oh God. Good news or bad news?

The guy grins.

                    GUY
I saw "Kenneth Lonergan,"
"Chekhov," and even "Shakespeare"
scribbled down. So do with that
information what you will.

CHAPTER SEVEN

When my junior year came to an end, I rather thrillingly chose to spend summer break doing things that would look good on college applications. There was an experimental museum in the hills off East Hollywood that offered free courses to high-performing public-school students, classes like Seminar on Creativity, and How to Think Like a Genius, Even If You Aren't One.

I enrolled in Life Experience 101, in part out of a burning curiosity over what on God's earth that could mean, but also because I was genuinely in search of what the class claimed to offer. The course met twice a week at the museum's hillside building, a boxy architectural wonder that opened up onto a lush lawn on one side and a man-made ravine on the other. I walked into the classroom on the first day, and a slight, goateed man eagerly shook my hand. "I'm Victor," he said. "Take a seat up front, and we'll get started in a minute."

I grabbed a chair in between a long-haired kid in a *Tron* T-shirt and a petite Filipina girl with a Hello Kitty backpack. I pulled out my notebook and looked around the room. My eyes came to rest on the class's second instructor, who sat quietly near the front of the room, flipping through a book. He was a handsome but worn-in guy in his late twenties with closely cropped hair and tattoos covering both arms. His scuffed boots were kicked up onto the table in front of him, and one of his arms rested casually on top of a sleek motorcycle helmet.

"Welcome to your summer adventure," Victor said, pausing for applause that never came. "As you know, I'm Victor."

He pointed to the other teacher. "And this here is Blake Ableton, an accomplished visual artist and world traveler."

The handsome teacher offered a Scout salute and a little smirk. "Yo," he said.

Victor continued to tout the virtues of Blake, explaining that the younger teacher had grown up on a farm and knew how to do things like milk cows and clean up after hogs. Gritting his teeth, Blake seemed to barely tolerate the explanation, clearly not vying to jump on a horse and ride back home to Iowa anytime soon. Victor then asked each of us to stand and offer an unexpected fact about ourselves. When it was my turn, I walked to the front of the room and offered the dumbest fact about myself I could think of, hoping it would make Blake laugh.

"I am a proud member of the Cherokee Nation," I said solemnly. "A full sixteenth on my father's side."

· · ·

At the start of the second class, we were each handed a Polaroid camera and a pack of film, and let loose to photograph three found objects and invent their backstories. I stuck close to the grounds, looking for pieces of trash that might contain the meaning of life as laid out by Aristotle, or at least a decently compelling plastic action figure. I rejected a filthy beach towel and a sneaker before coming across a deflating balloon tied to a tree. I snapped my shot and shook the photo, to make sure it would develop, before I moved on.

As I rounded the corner, I spotted Blake through the trees, leaned up against a chain-link fence that cordoned the grounds off from the dirty ravine. He was smoking a cigarette and idly kicking pebbles through the fence. I watched him for a minute before I slowly mean-dered over, posturing as though I were searching for something to pho-tograph. I put the camera up to my eye and looked through it, then rejected the composition. When I was close enough to Blake that he couldn't ignore my presence, I pulled a cigarette from the full pack in my bag.

"Would you happen to have a lighter?"

The expression on Blake's face was an amused one, and he let it sting me for a moment before he reached into his pocket and handed me a plastic Bic bearing the image of a white wolf howling at the stars.

"Cool. Thanks."

I lit my smoke and handed the lighter back to Blake. I took a few steps toward the ravine and rested against the chain-link fence. Again, I put the Polaroid up to my eye but lowered it before snapping a photo. I drew a line in the dirt with the tip of my shoe and built up my courage.

"Hey." I turned back to Blake. "Can I see your lighter again?"

"Wow. Take it easy with the nicotine, kid," he said before tossing me the Bic.

I caught the lighter and examined it. I turned toward the fence and balanced the lighter between pieces of twisted metal so the head of the wolf was facing me. I stepped back. I put my Polaroid up to my eye and snapped a photo of the lighter in its new setting. Then I handed it back to Blake.

His eyebrows were raised in what I hoped was incredulity. At a dis-regard for the rules that was undeniably charming. "I don't think that's really the point of the exercise," was all he said.

"Um. Don't tell Victor?"

"All right. But you'd better come up with a damn good backstory for that lighter." Blake winked. He stomped out his cigarette and turned away. He slipped his hands into his pockets, and I watched him walk all the way back to the building. With one object left to photo-graph, I settled on a dirty tennis ball, thinking I could blow Victor's mind asunder by nailing the narrative of a scrappy, aged rottweiler.

The following week, Blake led the class for the first time, giving a talk on how to translate real-world experiences into art. He had prepared a slide show of his paintings and the seemingly incongruous scenes that had inspired them. A month spent living in a tiny apartment in Mexico City begat photographs of shoeless boys playing soccer in the grimy streets, and old toothless men surrounded by bottles of tequila. But the paintings Blake created were less literal interpretations of the photos and more oily abstractions imbued with a similar sense of motion. The point he was making was pretty obvious, but the artwork was nice to look at, and I wanted to appear as fully absorbed in the presentation as I possibly could, so I scooted my chair forward and hardly allowed myself to blink.

Blake took us through the backwoods of Kentucky and the metropolises of South America, then showed the bodies of work inspired by each place. He paused as he flipped to the next batch of slides. "I was on the fence about showing you guys this set," he said. "But Victor convinced me you're all mature enough to handle it."

He scrolled through images of rural Thailand that quickly turned into cityscapes and portraits of people shopping at a busy market. Then we were inside a nightclub and out into a dark alley lit by a string of lanterns. The final and most potent photo depicted two young girls, probably prostitutes and definitely jailbait, sitting naked on the end of a foldout bed. The following image—ostensibly inspired by the last—showed one of Blake's paintings, an abstraction containing bamboo-like strips of paint over various free-floating anonymous body parts cut from porno mags. The class looked at the painting for several seconds before half the room erupted into spontaneous giggles.

"Cool," Blake said. "Victor, you were definitely right about the maturity level here."

Blake switched off the projector, obviously pissed. The presentation turned into a discussion about how to interpret interpretation—but seeing as it was led by Victor and not Blake, I let myself check out. I lingered a little after the session was over, swallowing a booster in the women's bathroom and fixing my eye makeup. I walked slowly to the parking lot and took my time unlocking the door of my car. Eventually, I saw Blake heading down the steps and waved, waiting to see if he'd come over. He did.

"Hey," I said. "I really liked your thing today."

"Yeah? Thanks. I never know how people are going to react to that stuff."

"It was interesting. And it made sense. I mean, it finally felt like there was a reason I'd signed up for this class."

"Oh?" Blake raised his eyebrows. "Do you not feel like you've gained invaluable experience in the ways of life?"

I laughed a little harder than I meant to. "Hey, can I ask why you're teaching this class? I mean, besides today, you haven't seemed all that into it. No offense."

"None taken, I guess."

"Sorry," I said. "That was stupid of me."

Blake looked over his shoulder to make sure no one was around. He leaned forward. "Okay, honestly? It's part of a community-service deal."

"For real?"

"I mean, I get paid too, so two birds, one stone."

"Oh. So what did you . . . do?"

"DUI. Smashed a telephone pole up pretty bad. And half my ribs. But I probably shouldn't be telling you this."

"Did you go to jail?"

"Briefly."

"So it's just community service now?"

"And court-mandated Alcoholics Anonymous. But I'm *certain* I shouldn't be telling you that."

"So you don't drink?"

"Six months sober."

"I think I'm supposed to say congratulations?"

Blake laughed again. "You can say whatever you want."

He shot me another of his patented winks and walked away. But our precarious almost-friendship was sealed, which translated to me helping him pack up his stuff and take it to his car at the end of every class. Once Life Experience 101 came to an end (with a final assignment to interview a homeless person—as luck would have it, mine turned out to be the world's foremost authority on chemtrails), I convinced Blake to take me on as a studio intern, selling the internship as a thing I could put down on college apps. A few nights a week, I'd go over to the work space he shared with three other artists. I'd help him prep materials and grind fiberglass for his multimedia paintings.

"This is a really great one," I'd offer pretty much every time he finished a work.

Sometimes our hands would brush while stretching a canvas, and I'd find myself suddenly forced to take a sharp inhalation of oxygen. We didn't talk a ton on those nights but worked with diligence peppered by occasional banter. On smoke breaks on the fire escape, I would mock Blake for his persona as a sensitive artiste, and he would make fun of me for being a dumb teenager.

I always tried to limit my drug intake on nights I spent at Blake's studio, ostensibly concerned it would mess with his sobriety, but really, worried he would judge me and no longer want to hang out.

One day I came to the studio straight from a full day of working on a new play and was artificially amped to a pretty insane degree. I knew instantly that Blake could tell I was high, although he never brought it up directly. "You feeling okay?" he asked at one point while I mixed paint together like I was beating a stubborn egg.

"Oh yeah," I said. "Totally. I had way too much coffee earlier."

"Then I definitely won't offer you any more."

I tried to steady my hands enough to prime a canvas. I was feeling bouncy but even more productive than usual. I could feel Blake watching me, and I couldn't help but notice that he seemed curious about the chemicals floating around inside my body. We worked until dawn, at which point he told me he was heading out to Mexico to gather some inspiration, but should be back in a few days. He ended up staying gone for two weeks.

. . .

I spent fourteen straight nights hovering by the phone, waiting for Blake to call. When he finally did, his words were wobbly and he kept laughing at some untold joke. Still, I was thrilled when he asked me to come over to his studio that night, and wasted the evening trying on and discarding outfits until I looked suitably cool—but not like I was trying to be cool, of course.

I could smell alcohol on his breath before I'd even crossed the room. An empty bottle of Jack Daniel's was pushed underneath a chair. I settled in to work, but I couldn't stop sneaking glances to see what he was doing.

"What's up?" he asked after I'd shot half a dozen big-eyed inquiries in his direction.

"Is it okay that you're drinking?"

"Yeah," he said. "I mean, my probation's up."

"Oh, cool." It sounded reasonable to me, and who was I to moralize about sobriety. "I mean . . . I think I'm supposed to say congratulations?"

Blake laughed. He was trying to finish a painting, a large abstract work on plexiglass, but it was clear his heart wasn't in it. And he was acting more than a little jumpy. "Hey," he said, putting down his brush. "You want to get out of here?"

I smiled and gave him a thumbs-up, trying to contain the influx of excitement that was filling my veins.

Blake drove me to a little bar called Freddy's that was stashed away on the east side of town. He shook hands with the bouncer, and the roly-poly tough guy allowed me to walk in without showing ID. "Long time, brother," the guy said.

"Yeah, I've been out of town," Blake said quickly, avoiding my eyes.

Blake got us drinks, and we headed to the pool table at the back of the bar, where we swiftly learned that neither of us could play worth a damn. But we fucked around with the equipment anyway, and after a million misses I took the lead, simply because I was the one with the least blurry eyesight. We put music on the jukebox and tried to entice one another into betting on our game.

"Okay," I said. "If I win, I get to keep the painting with the floating body parts."

"And if I win," Blake said, "you have to clean my whole studio."

"If I win, you have to make me dinner."

"If I win, we come back here tomorrow."

The bartender offered us a round of shots, so we set down our cues and guzzled more booze. I could feel the whiskey burn its way down my throat and then travel back up to cushion my brain. We took a smoke break on the patio, and Blake had to steady himself by leaning up against the railing. He smiled at me. I flipped him off. Blake swayed a little as he smoked his cigarette down to the filter.

"You're so pretty," he slurred.

I shook my head as if to say *What a sap*, but took the compliment and stashed it away somewhere secure. I stomped out my smoke and walked back into the bar, where I picked up my pool cue. Blake watched me intently as we played the next few rounds. We both got drunker and drunker, which somehow actually improved our pool skills. I used my cue to shoot the white ball so that the last of my colored balls went into the hole, and raised my hands in triumph.

"Congratulations, champ-yon," Blake said with a thick tongue. He slunk over to me. He took me by the hand and pulled me into the dark hallway. He walked me up against the wall and started kissing me everywhere but on my lips. He sucked at my neck and pressed his hands up and down my body.

"Is this okay?" he asked.

"Yeah," I said, and Blake shoved his tongue in my mouth and mashed his forehead up against my own. It was exactly what I'd wanted for weeks, but I couldn't stifle the feeling that this night wasn't going to form a happy memory.

"Hey." His breath was hot in my ear. "Let's get high."

What should have been music to my ears sounded more like an alarm bell. Nevertheless, I beckoned Blake into the women's room and crushed up a few Adderall. Blake smacked his hands across his cheeks and let out a whoop.

"Now let's find real drugs," Blake said, and I nodded my compliance.

He pulled out his phone and left the bathroom. When I walked out shortly after, he grabbed my hand and headed for the front door, very much in a hurry.

"Where are we going?" I asked.

"My place. The guy's meeting us there."

Blake sped through side streets, making abrupt turns that forced me to grab hold of the door handle to avoid falling out of my seat. I wanted to tell him to slow down but figured it wouldn't make a difference. He took us up a dark road just a stone's throw from the freeway. He parked his car and told me to wait inside. He got out and crossed the street, where he slipped into the passenger side of an idling lowrider. A minute later, he was back and beckoning me to follow him up to his apartment.

Blake unlocked the front door but didn't turn on the lights, letting the space remain illuminated solely by streetlamps filtered through his flimsy curtains. The place was tiny and bleak. It contained very little furniture, and all the dishes were being used as ashtrays. There was no proper bed, just a mattress on the floor, barely covered by a black sheet. The walls were decorated sparsely with taped-up pencil sketches and magazine tear-outs. I looked around without turning my head and took in the disappointment of the apartment.

Blake grabbed two beers out of his otherwise empty fridge and pulled a clear baggie filled with sharp white crystals from his pocket.

He held it out for me to examine, in a gesture so reverent I wondered if he thought he was looking at a plastic bag full of diamonds.

"Is that . . . meth?" I asked

"Fuck yes," Blake said. "You'll love it."

I was drunk and dizzy, and I wanted to brush my teeth. There was a whiskey stain on my shirt and the smell of tobacco in my hair. Those were things I knew for certain. But whether I felt like smoking crystal meth with my summer-school teacher in a dark, decrepit apartment on the edge of Los Angeles was something I wasn't sure about one way or the other.

Blake rummaged around in a drawer until he found a burned-up glass pipe. He placed some of the crystals inside and pulled out his white-wolf lighter. He held the flame beneath the pipe until the bulb bubbled and glowed like a gaseous planet. Then he placed the pipe up to his lips and inhaled, releasing chemical warfare back into the room. He took another hit and passed me the pipe. I followed suit, letting the burning crystals rocket their way inside me. I exhaled and coughed loudly.

"Take another hit," Blake said.

I paused my hacking to inhale more chemicals, then swiftly resumed with doubled intensity. Blake grabbed the pipe back from me and put it up to his mouth. He bounced up and down on the balls of his feet and put his hands on my shoulders. Everything inside me felt taut and acute, like my body had been taken in for a tune-up, and my wires were accidentally tightened too much. There was pleasure flowing through me, but my brain was becoming confused by an overload of sensations. Blake shoved me up against the wall and kissed me. I couldn't tell if it was what I wanted, but I couldn't just stand there while my head unraveled, so I closed my eyes and let Blake gnash his teeth against me and claw at my jeans.

He had my shirt off, and then he stopped, overtaken by a sudden burst of clarity. I didn't want to have a conversation, and I needed somewhere to put my energy. So I unbuttoned his pants, which was all he needed to flip me onto the spartan mattress and do the same with mine. There was sweat and spit everywhere, and my head was inches from a makeshift ashtray. My body felt like it might explode or shut off or simply walk out of the room and leave my consciousness behind. With Blake on top of me as dawn crept through the curtains, I wished for the first time in my life that I were someone else.

Blake shut his eyes and thrust into me. I tried to push my arms against his chest in the hopes it would make him slow down, but he was operating inside some sort of fugue state. I bit down on my hand to keep from whimpering. Finally, Blake rolled off of me and flopped over to the other side of the mattress, breathing heavily. There were red marks from my own teeth on my hand, and scratches from Blake all over my body.

I pulled the black sheet over myself and tried to think of something to say. But Blake wouldn't look at me, and I could see him fighting inside his own head. He got up and filled a glass with tap water. He drained it in one gulp and then filled it again. He got a beer from the fridge and popped it open. Then he handed me the glass.

As I downed the acrid water, Blake went back for his pipe and the bag of crystal. I didn't want to watch, so I turned my head toward the window. Soon, Blake was hopping all around the room. The fight inside his head appeared to have been subdued. He sat down on the mattress and offered me the pipe, but I shook my head.

"Come on," he said. "Don't bail on me now. Let's just talk. And hang out."

"Honestly, I think I've probably had enough of that."

"Oh, great."

"I meant the meth. Obviously."

"You barely smoked any."

"I just feel kind of weird."

"Whatever," Blake said. "I thought you were like me."

He almost had me with the accusation, and he could tell. He held the pipe out in front of me, just over my head. He smiled. I nearly took it, but panic began to rise inside my stomach, and I shook my head.

"It's late," I said. "So late it's early."

"What is that, teenage poetry?"

"Oh, fuck you."

"Come on, I'm just kidding."

Blake reached out to touch me, and I recoiled. I was on edge and needed to leave. I stood and put my clothes on. The sun was up, and I realized I didn't have my car. I fought back tears as I hurriedly threw my hair into a ponytail. Blake shrugged. He sank back onto the mattress and took another hit of the meth. He mumbled something under his breath, and then said it again more loudly to be sure I'd hear it. "That's what I get for fucking little babies."

The space behind my eyes went white, and I bit down on my tongue, determined I wouldn't let Blake see me cry. I felt crazy and sticky and completely in over my head.

"You are an asshole," I said. "And a creep."

"Hey," he said through a cloud of chemicals as I headed for the door. "You're the one who wanted the fucking life experience."

I ran out of the apartment and paced the block. I took a deep breath and forced my brain to function. I called Mari and begged her to come pick me up. She'd been sleeping, and it took a minute for her to even understand what I was asking. But I couldn't hide the quiver in my voice, and she promised to bring her chariot to me posthaste as soon as she realized I might actually be in trouble.

I walked a few blocks to sit in the parking lot of a donut shop so I wouldn't have to be totally honest about where I'd been all night. After twenty endless minutes, Mari pulled up and blasted her horn. "Hey, weirdo, get in."

"Is it okay if we don't talk about it?" I asked right away.

Mari looked me over. "You okay?"

"Yeah."

She paused for a moment and considered whether I was telling the truth. "Then, bitch, you better buy me a donut for my trouble."

I put all my gratitude into a grin. I walked into the shop and came out with half a dozen pastries, which Mari inhaled and I picked at while she drove me to my car. But the donuts weren't cutting it. From the second I'd left Blake's apartment, all I could think about was going home and immediately ingesting something that would allow me to twist the memory of the night into something else altogether.

INT. INDUSTRIAL WAREHOUSE — NIGHT

A rave is in full effect. Music throbs. People wander
around, dancing and waving glow sticks. There's quite a
bit of touching going on, most of it MDMA-induced.

In a corner, we see Leila, alone and looking flushed.
She downs a bottle of water and drops it. It lands on
top of a GUY who's lying on the floor and smiling up at
the ceiling.

                    LEILA
                 (muttering)
          Sorry.

Leila wanders to the back patio, where there's more
touching and a lot of smoking. She walks over to an
INDUSTRIAL KID in combat boots. He has a pacifier around
his neck and is holding a pack of menthols.

                    LEILA
          Hi. Can I . . . ?

The kid smiles and hands Leila a cigarette, which he
lights. Then he runs a hand through her hair.

Leila walks away.

                 INDUSTRIAL KID
          Hey, where you going?

Leila slumps against a wall and smokes her cigarette,
staring out. A second later, two bodies slide down on
either side of her. It's Mari and Devon.

                         DEVON
             We've been looking all over for
             you.

                         LEILA
             I feel fucking weird.

                         MARI
             Yeah, you don't look so great, bud.

They sit silently for a moment.

                         DEVON
             Mari made out with some old guy.

                         MARI
             Whatever. He had water. And candy.

                         LEILA
             Werther's Originals?

Devon laughs. He puts his arm around Leila's shoulder,
and they stare out at the spectacle before them.

CHAPTER EIGHT

As soon as I turned seventeen, I acquired a nemesis. A mortal enemy and a true foe. Her name was Lulu.

To explain: my biggest problem during this period was sleep. I usually didn't need much of it, found it just got in the way, but there were times my body simply refused to function at the level I was demanding of it. And when that happened, I had no choice but to push my drugs aside (like, inches; somewhere easily retrievable come the first nauseating rays of sunlight) and surrender to my pillow and my CD of chirping crickets. However, sleep didn't always accept such a quick white flag; it wanted to battle a little more and earn its victory. And so, with my official army of uppers unable to soldier on, I was forced to call in reinforcements—in the form of benzos and opiates.

Though a steady supply of Ritalin and Adderall was easy to come by in my universe of overmedicated teens, downers tended to fall more squarely in the realm of adult problem-solvers. So I began to raid the cabinets of my friends' parents for those sweet tablets of dreamland bliss. It was a simple solution to a big problem; or so it would have been if it weren't for Lulu.

Lulu was my age and weighed about ninety pounds. She had wispy blonde hair that wrapped around her tiny skull in a single braid. She wore flowy skirts and Victorian corsets, like an Ophelia interpreted by Courtney Love. Opiates were Lulu's main thing—those and the clove cigarettes she smoked constantly while buzzing around in the concentric circles that made up her own little world.

Despite this other-planetary weirdness, Lulu was gifted with the innate ability to arrive at parties exactly ten minutes before I did—which meant she could hit the master bathroom first and leave me a beggar for medicine-cabinet scraps. Time after time, I'd put in half an hour of gabbing about that Rilo Kiley show at the Fonda last month only to make my escape to the upstairs bathroom and find it already plundered of all its lovely Rx nectars. Sometimes Lulu would show a little mercy and leave me a pill or two, smirking as she floated through the bathroom door, but she usually emptied the place for all it was worth—a level that even I had not yet sunk to. Hollywood mothers need their Valium, after all.

Lulu's and my little game of pharmaceutical fencing came to a head one night at a party held on the last night of Thanksgiving break. Mari bailed at the last minute to go drop acid at Disneyland with her new boyfriend, so I arrived at the grand Spanish colonial house all by my lonesome. I was halfway across the dining room when my eyes landed on Lulu—once again, she had beaten me there. She appeared to be somewhat integrated into the crowd, but I could tell she still had a bit of mingling to do before she could make her way up to the bathroom without drawing suspicion.

"Leila, hey!"

I felt a tap on my shoulder and spun around to see a beblazered guy named Carter, looking bloated from his first few months of college.

"Wow, it's good to see you." I gave him a hug, and we walked over to the beverage table. "How's Brown?"

"Brown's okay," Carter said, sucking a Sam Adams. "I was kind of expecting a little more stimulation, you know? But everyone's more into beer than Baudrillard."

"Maybe you just haven't found your crowd. Look for a guy in a black turtleneck and crack a joke—if he laughs, run in the other direction."

"Don't mock me, Massey. This is going to be you in just one short year. Unless you've already landed yourself an honorary PhD. I wouldn't be surprised."

"Is a PhD that thing that gets you out of living in dorms? If so, sign me up."

Lulu had slowly edged her way to the bottom of the stairs. She was getting pretty close to the point where she'd be able to casually turn and float up them, undeterred by her pointy-toed lace-up boots. But she wasn't quite there yet. She still had to sufficiently bore a skinny twerp in a popped collar into fumbling for an excuse and bailing on their conversation.

As for me, I was going to have to pull a move a bit more drastic from my arsenal of shithead tactics.

I'd never had much of a taste for vodka, but this wasn't the time to turn all liquor connoisseur. While Carter rambled on about the intricacies of Ivy League dining halls, I poured myself a splash of Absolut topped off with a full helping of cranberry juice. I slowly spread my stance wider so as to make myself more in the way, nodding at Carter's culinary pontifications all the while. "Nothing but french fries for lunch does sound brutal," I said.

When a girl in a Guns N' Roses tee squeezed herself in half to get by me, I made my move. I turned hard into Carter and tilted my cup, splashing the drink down my own dress.

"Shit," I yelled, making sure to call all of the room's attention to myself.

"Oh my God. Did I do that to you?" Carter interrupted his speech on Rhode Island's paucity of fake meat products to worry over his role in my brand-new stain.

"No—it's okay," I said, yanking a paper towel and gesturing upstairs. "I'm just gonna clean up . . ."

Before I darted off, my eyes locked with Carter's for just a second, and I saw how genuinely awful he felt—which in turn did a number on my own conscience. But it wasn't the time for such concerns.

I wasted no time sweeping right past Lulu—whose mouth dropped open when she saw me—and dashing up the stairs. I heard a snippet of her conversation with the human popped collar as I passed: "My uncle set up a meeting with Russell Simmons's personal assistant. So I've just got to impress that guy with my beats and—"

A click, like entry into heaven. I locked the bathroom door and ran both faucets, creating a little symphony of splashes. Then I wiggled open the medicine cabinet and took inventory: toothpaste; dental picks; unopened Bayer aspirin; hemorrhoid cream; a bottle of Percocet, fairly recent; and one of Vicodin, expired. I emptied all but two of the Vics into an old Advil bottle I'd brought along, figuring that if they were expired, no one would miss them. I stole only half the Percocets, because my application for sainthood was still pending.

I closed the medicine cabinet and caught sight of my reflection in its mirrored door. The cranberry juice had seeped into the fibers of my gray shirtdress, pooling into a big red stain around my heart. With a little finessing I could sell the look to a boutique on Melrose.

I splashed some water onto my shirt and shut off the faucet. Making my way back down the stairs, I affected my best long-suffering-young-woman-surrounded-by-cavemen look. The added bonus to this little maneuver was that I didn't even have to stay for the rest of the party. I could beg off, citing wardrobe catastrophe, and head home for some desperately needed drugged-up shut-eye. I darted through the crowd, waving quick good-byes to a few friends. Carter ran up and grabbed my hand. "I feel like such a jerk," he said. "Let me take you to dinner to make up for it. There's a new vegan place on Sunset."

My gaze somersaulted downward to spotlight the stain on my dress.

"Here," Carter said, shedding his blazer. "You can wear my jacket."

"Seriously, it's not a big deal at all. But I am kind of sticky, so I should go bathe myself. We'll do something while you're in town though, yeah?"

Carter nodded, looking mildly crushed, and I breezed out the front door and up the block. I was almost at my car when I heard a shrill, floaty voice calling out to me. "Bitch."

I ignored it and kept walking.

"Hey, bitch, wait up."

I turned and saw Lulu walking over to me, as fast as she could muster. She was breathing heavily. "Leila, right?"

"Hi, Lulu."

"That was a nice move you pulled back there," she squeaked, and I saw desperation in her eyes. Here was a new, up-close Lulu, flesh and blood and not quite the hazy dead-flower child I encountered on verandas in the Valley. "But now you're gonna hand over what you took."

I laughed. *Are you serious, you little nut job?* But she was, as it turned out, entirely too serious. Lulu opened her hand and revealed a small silver switchblade. She flipped it open and pointed it right at me. "Like I said, Leila. You're going to give me what you took."

The situation was surreal. It was unnerving, of course, but also bizarrely hilarious to watch this tiny polka dot of a teenage rich girl threaten me with a knife that had probably belonged to one of the Stone Temple Pilots. I doubted she'd use it, but I couldn't be sure—the panic in her irises was all too vivid. "Give. Me. What. You. Got."

A few kids stumbled out onto the street, drunk from the party, but they were too busy trying to stay upright to notice me and Lulu. I heard one of them slur, "Nah, we'll have to go through the Valley. DUI checkpoints are all over the Hollywood side of Mulholland."

Lulu didn't turn around; she just continued to point her little knife into the air.

"Okay, okay," I started, watching the tiny girl carefully, but not quite willing to abandon my goal of a good night's rest. "Look, I understand. You really want your pills. And so do I. Put the knife down, and I'll give you half of what I grabbed. Okay?"

Lulu kept the knife aimed in my direction. Her whole frail-little-bird body was shaking. Then she nodded and lowered the blade. I slowly pulled the Advil bottle from my bag and emptied half the bounty into my hand. I transferred the pills into Lulu's palm, which was ice-cold and a whiter-than-white shade of pale. She popped a couple and looked at me.

"You, uh, want a ride or something?" I asked. Lulu shook her head and pointed to a light-pink bicycle with skull-patterned streamers on the handles and a dirty, eyeless teddy bear in the basket.

From that point on, Lulu and I worked out an arrangement. Without ever speaking again, every time we were at the same house party, one of us would slip half her score to the other. We went on like that for the rest of the year, handshaking Percocets across a throng of clueless teenagers, until Lulu gradually faded away from the scene. I left too, but the invisible ink she'd been pumping into her veins took hold first. I heard rumors Lulu had made good at rehab, but I could have sworn I saw her with her hand inside a junkie musician's pants in a hotel room in Vegas half a decade later, as thin as ever in that same tattered dress.

CHAPTER NINE

There wasn't anything about the idea of attending my senior prom that appealed to me—pastel gowns, group dances, smiling—but I got talked into it by Jasper, the Disney star pal of my ex-fling Griffin. He and Jessika had broken up (picnic, threesome), and Jasper started hounding me to hang out.

Jasper had recently moved on from the late-afternoon world of Disney shows to the early-night universe of CW shows. He starred as Hunter Hunt on *Hunter's Point*, a coming-of-age tale about a New York City rich kid who's sent off to live with his grandmother in Hunter, Maine. The production was gearing up to shoot its prom episode, and Jasper was suddenly hit by a wave of remorse that he'd never been able to attend his own high-school galas, three years earlier. So he called me up. "Leila, important question: Would you like to go to your prom with me?"

"Hell no," I replied before asking if he had any coke.

But Jasper persisted, and I finally broke down, telling him I'd take him to the dance on the condition that he find another handsome young television star to be Mari's date, as she'd just been dumped midway through a bad mushroom trip at Magic Mountain. He snapped up Cullen Cuse, a blond former model who played a teen ghost on a different CW hour-long, and the four of us set off to experience an American tradition.

Our prom was held at the Gene Autry museum in Burbank, a weird little tribute venue to the late Singing Cowboy. I'll admit I was vaguely excited by the prospect of a Western-themed dance. However, the brilliant teenage minds of the event committee decided that the motif should be "One Night in Paris" instead. So bronze stallions were replaced with cardboard cutouts of the Eiffel Tower, American Indians were given berets, and we were served a dinner of rock-solid steak frites.

Nevertheless, my gang arrived in style. Jasper rented a limo for the four of us, and we spread out in the back, armed with bottles of Dom Pérignon and mountains of cocaine. By the time we hit the freeway, Mari was in Cullen's lap, playing with his blond locks and grilling him. "So, okay," she said. "You're a ghost, but other people can see you?"

"Yeah, but just other teenagers. No adults. So, like, the teachers? I don't exist for them."

"Then why do you go to school?"

"Because I like it, I guess? I mean, what else would I do all day?"

"I don't know—live in a castle and haunt people?"

"There's not a lot of room for episode arcs in a castle, baby."

Jasper was snapping photos of us with a throwaway camera he'd picked up at Rite-Aid. Instead of the standard prom photos posed in parents' backyards, our memories were to be of drinking and groping in the backseat of a rented vehicle. The camera's flash went off in my eyes just as I was swilling straight from a bottle of Dom.

Instead of parking in the lot like the yellow flyer of prom rules dictated (no alcohol, obscene attire, or using the dance as an excuse to neglect those term papers, dang it), Jasper had our rent-a-chauffeur drop us right in front of the museum. It was as if we were arriving at a ball thrown in our very honor, and Jasper was so excited he momentarily stopped complaining that I'd forgotten to get him a boutonniere. I stepped out of the car wearing a lacy black corset-top gown and a pair of three-inch heels. Mari was more demure, in a cherry-red minidress accented by the world's most convincing push-up bra. Our fellows were suited up in designer tuxes, and their hair was perfectly coiffed around their pretty TV faces.

"Good luck trying to play a ghost here," Mari told Cullen as the boys were swarmed by a flock of starstruck teenage girls.

"Will you sign my corsage?" one of them screeched. "What about my retainer?"

After a couple of minutes spent watching our dates scramble, Mari and I rescued them, and we made our way through the doors of the museum. Fake streetlamps and paper stars transformed the room into a kindergartner's sketch of the Rue de la Paix. Incongruous reggaeton played to a cluster of dressed-up bodies swaying on the dance floor. The pimply teens of third-period AP Biology were out en masse, transformed by silk and chiffon for one night only.

"I need a pick-me-up," I said to Jasper. He grabbed my hand and spun me around, transferring his vial of cocaine into my palm.

The evening passed in a blur of trips to the bathroom, trips to sneak cigarettes with Mari, and trips to steal my date away from CW fans who wanted him to autograph various body parts. Late into the night, Jasper finally succeeded in luring me in for a slow dance. Nothing physical had ever happened between us, but with his hand on the small of my back and our feet stepping in time to Green Day's most lethargic effort, I felt like tonight was probably our chance to take advantage of all that French romance in the air. "You having fun?" I asked, and in response, Jasper twirled me around and around.

There was an after-party at a hotel downtown, but we had other plans. Jasper had booked the penthouse at the Roosevelt Hotel, and the four of us headed over, buzzing on the hyperreality of the night. More champagne waited inside, along with a dozen long-stemmed roses. "Planning on making this a prom to remember?" I teased Jasper, pushing him playfully.

"Oui, oui, mademoiselle," he replied.

We popped open the bottle of booze, spread out what was left of our blow, and turned on the radio. Mari and Cullen were waltzing around the room in imitation of the goons who'd just sullied the dance floor of the Autry museum. I plopped down on the bed and burned eye contact into Jasper. He started toward me but was intercepted by a sky-high Cullen, who was looping around in circles and wiping white residue from his nose. "Aren't we supposed to play, like, spin the bottle or something?" Cullen asked.

"Dude, there are only four of us," Jasper said.

"What about truth or dare?"

"I'm in," I said, pouring a glass of champagne and sitting down on the floor next to Mari.

"Okay then, Leila," Jasper said as we formed a circle on the carpet. "Truth or dare?"

"Truth, motherfucker."

"Have you ever made a sex tape?"

"No idea."

"Come on."

"Seriously, I can't remember. Probably? Maybe one time with Griffin—he *was* really into photography."

"That's a bullshit answer." Jasper sighed. "But it's your turn."

"Cullen, pick your poison."

"The manly choice is obviously 'dare.'"

"I dare you to make out with Jasper."

Cullen hesitated for only a second before yanking Jasper's head toward him and shoving his tongue down the other actor's throat. When they pulled back a few seconds later, Mari and I treated them to a round of applause.

"You're a pretty good kisser, Cull," Jasper said. "But I think that should count as my turn too."

I leaned over Jasper to inhale a line of blow. "Fine. Ask away."

"Mari," Jasper said, turning toward the beauty in the red dress sitting to his right. "Truth . . . or dare?"

"I know you're totally gonna ask me and Leila to kiss, and I want to torture you," she said, spreading cocaine along her gums. "So truth."

"First fuck?" Jasper asked, grinning slyly at Mari. She tensed up suddenly. She shrugged, as if to say *I don't remember.*

"What's wrong with the memories on you chicks?" Cullen asked. "Do you both have early-onset Alzheimer's?"

"Come on," Jasper prodded. "You have to know who took your virginity."

"I was drunk," Mari replied.

"Wait—I know that story," I said. "You seriously don't remember?"

"You tell it then."

"Mari got down with this kid Hamilton who lives around the corner. She was, like, fifteen, and he was a ginger. Remember now?"

Mari nodded and took a swill from the bottle of Dom.

"No, no," Jasper said, stopping her. "That's not right, is it, Mari?"

"Oh shit," Cullen chimed in. "Mari has a dirty secret."

"Well, come on then, out with it. Rules are rules. Who was the lucky fella who got to mar Mari?"

"My stepfather."

Jasper and Cullen laughed, sure she was joking.

"When I was fourteen."

They shut up abruptly, realizing she wasn't.

"It wasn't like, you know . . . I mean, it was consensual."

I looked at Mari, but she wouldn't meet my eyes. A heavy silence descended over our circle, spotlighting the Iggy Pop song playing from the stereo. Here was my best friend in the world, the person ostensibly closer to me than anyone, and it turns out I didn't know the most basic thing about her. I'd been too concerned with pills and dusts and test scores to bother with actual human beings.

I went out to the balcony to smoke a cigarette. A minute later Mari joined me, yanking an American Spirit from the pack in my hand.

"Hey," she said. "Are you mad I didn't tell you?"

"Nah, I just feel like a jerk. If you thought you couldn't, or whatever."

"It's just weird, you know?"

I lit Mari's cigarette, and she inhaled for what seemed like minutes. Then she released the smoke from her lungs, and we both watched it escape in one tight puff that slowly disseminated outward and upward toward the stars.

I wrapped my arms around her. "Hey, Mari? Remember that day you had to pick me up at the donut shop? How come you never asked me about that?"

"You said you didn't want to talk about it."

"Can I talk about it now?"

"Of course."

Mari and I sat down on the balcony, turning our chairs so they faced each other. I told her about Blake, about him breaking his sobriety by downing drink after drink, and then about the meth. Mari just listened. The poker face she'd been perfecting for years didn't betray whether she was surprised by the story, and I didn't have much to say about it other than a revelation of the stark, brutal facts. Still, I felt marginally better after putting it out there, realizing that sharing a story is one way to make the pain it bears start to disappear. It was a lesson I'd learn over and over again, as I'd amass different versions of the same agonizing experience for years to come.

But for one night, I felt better. After talking for hours, Mari and I curled up against one another in the master bed, still in our prom dresses, leaving the boys to make do with the disappointing familiarity of their own bodies.

INT. HOSPITAL EXAM ROOM - DAY

Leila vomits into the sink, then sits down on the exam
table. Her hair is a mess, and her eye makeup smeared.

A knock and then a FILIPINO DOCTOR enters. He immediately spots the mess in the sink and bites his lip.

                    DOCTOR
          Okay, Miss Massey. What brought you
          here today?

                    LEILA
          I keep throwing up. I can't stop.

                    DOCTOR
          How long has this been going on?

                    LEILA
          Six hours. Maybe seven.

The doctor looks Leila over.

                    DOCTOR
          And what did you take?

She pauses a moment.

                    LEILA
          Um, I had a few beers. And a friend
          gave me a Vicodin, I think. Is that
          what they're called? I didn't real-
          ize the combination would make me
          so sick.

                    DOCTOR
Anything else in your system?

                    LEILA
No. It was a stupid mistake. No
more of that for me.

                    DOCTOR
And can I ask where you consumed
these substances?

                    LEILA
A party. At a friend's house. We're
all going off to college, so it was
a big celebration. I know better
now, and I'll never do it again.

The doctor looks at Leila for another second and
sighs. Then goes to his prescription pad and starts to
scribble.

CHAPTER TEN

The fedora is a creased felt hat worn usually by men, sometimes by women. The name comes from an 1882 play by French dramatist Victorien Sardou—called, appropriately enough, *Fédora*—in which the female protagonist spent her stage time prancing about in a topper very similar to what is now labeled the "fedora." Thus, a grand linguistic leap was made. The hat is often associated with the Prohibition era, the Depression era, private detectives in noir films, and young Hollywood assholes of two very distinct types.

The first breed of fedora asshole is a nightlife dude who prowls Sunset Boulevard with a skinny blonde on his arm and a pair of scuffed boots with the laces undone on his feet. His fedora is designer. He might be a commercial director, or he might be a stylist at Rudy's Barbershop who once produced a music video for a piano rock band. The second type of fedora douchebag pairs his hat, usually procured at Goodwill, with an oversized trench coat. He is pasty and doughy with stringy hair. He works at a niche video store and once wrote fan mail to Alfred Hitchcock's granddaughter. How do I know so much about fedoras? I attended USC film school, which happens to boast a rare ecosystem where both kinds of fedora assholes coexist in equal numbers. The fedora, I learned, is the secret scale upon which Hollywood balances.

USC also boasted such attractions as a sound design professor who used R2-D2 as a unit of measurement. As in "For the sound of the Apache chief's arrow whizzing past our hero's ear, the engineer recorded a Frisbee zooming over a gulch approximately as wide as ten R2-D2s."

There was an elderly French-Canadian screenwriting prof who'd forget what country he was in and occasionally trail off in a language no one understood. We were all pretty clear on the concept of the denouement, though—"class is over."

There was a grad student from a fancy Southern plantation family who used his thesis film to explore his own debilitating addiction to '70s pornography. There was a fistfight over Truffaut versus Godard. (No one won.) There was a female cinematography instructor who used her own work on a lesbian erotica film to demonstrate a lighting technique. (No one came.)

I was pursued by USC because of my sparkling glass table of a high-school academic record and my reputation as the teenage bard of Los Angeles. I was ceremoniously handed a partial scholarship. After a solid, responsible fifteen seconds of reflection, I decided to forgo a tiny shared room in the USC dorms, and I moved into an apartment in Silver Lake with Mari—who was taking a year off to find herself.

"This place could work," Mari said on the afternoon we went to check out the apartment. She stood in the living room and peered through the bars on the windows to get a look at the view.

"Definitely," I said, joining her at a window. The scenic highlight from the spot proved to be the signage on the liquor store down the street. "I mean, it's pretty nice, right?"

"Totally." Mari nodded. "It's amazing."

She was lying, of course. The place was a dump. The heat didn't work, there were mouse droppings in the cabinets, and a layer of filth had settled on top of every surface. But it didn't matter, because the

place was ours. The first day I moved in, I hired a teenage graffiti artist named Carlos, the younger brother of one of my new neighbors,
to paint a Virgen de Guadalupe mural on my bedroom wall—not a
religious thing but an offering to my new home on the east side of LA.
For years, the visage of this candy-colored mother of Christ was there
to tuck me into bed as the sun came up, my nose swollen and running
all over the books and scripts that shared my pillow. Later, she would
haunt me as I made my first of many attempts to grapple with the
demands of a rehab program.

· · ·

Like a lot of people who've been through twelve-step programs, I've
always had trouble with the third step, the one that asks you to recognize the existence of a higher power into whose sticky hands you're supposed to place your life. It's not the sheer existence of a God-type thing
I've had trouble conceiving—in fact, a pretty clear impression of this
highest of beings comes to mind pretty quickly. But that's the problem.
I can, in fact, envision a fully formed God—which only means that I
can't imagine anyone so complicated giving half a shit about me and
my problems.

In my mind, God lives in regimented detachment from the world
he created. He spends quiet mornings in the deepest recesses of nature
(no way God *hikes*, though), then swoops down to the suburbs to catch
a Little League game. He is stoic and introverted; he feels things deeply,
but he is quite cautious. This God weeps thunderstorms in front of
brick-red Rothkos, but he doesn't interfere with the bloody noses of an
amphetamine addict who once stole a bottle of Ritalin from the third
grader she was supposed to be teaching to read Roald Dahl.

Isn't this how you'd behave if you were God? It's how I would
operate for sure, but maybe that's why I'm the one with the debilitating addiction problem. In my experience, it has always been harder
to watch suffering than to bear it, although perhaps that's because the

bearer is able to turn away. And after some-fraction-of-infinity years spent watching over suffering, after seeing the repetition of the same old shitty patterns, the same flaws begetting the same flaws, a God who was in fact perfect would start to turn his gaze toward other things.

Folks often make use of the phrase "he's only human" to describe the little foibles that make up our daily lives—lashing out at a coworker during a hard afternoon at the office (as if I'd know anything about office work); forgetting to attend a friend's party; hiding copies of *Barely Legal Whatever-Turns-You-On* underneath the mattress. Implicit in the term "human" is contrast to the way a god would behave. So then God's infinitely free, yet still infinitely patient and infinitely compassionate? I don't buy it. Or rather, I give God a little more credit than that.

Maybe my problem is that if I'm going to imagine a higher power at all, I can only conceive of him in human terms. In fact, he sounds like a lot of the people in my life. So perhaps my subconscious is telling me that it's these folks I need to make peace with, to ask for help, and not God. But that's the ninth step.

Maybe my problem is that I've never been very good with order.

CHAPTER ELEVEN

As much as I liked setting up mousetraps in my new apartment and gazing out at the word "Liquor," most of my time was spent at school. My favorite spot on campus was the Marcia Lucas Post-Production Facility, which was truly my kind of joint. It was open all night and was a place where staring intently at one thing with Dyson-like focus for hours upon hours was actually encouraged.

One Wednesday around midnight, I headed to the edit room to work on the expletive-only David Mamet parody I had to finish by the end of the week. I was tired, but the idea of sitting down and crafting this video until it was as close to perfect as possible really appealed to me. There were a few other students in the room—an exhausted girl who wouldn't stop rubbing her eyes, a lanky guy who kept stepping outside to ingest Red Bulls, and Jed.

Jed was always in the edit room. He was working on a shot-by-shot re-creation of *Star Wars*, and his goal was to make it exactly like the original. He'd been at the project, his master's thesis, for two years. He waited for me to load my video up, then called me over. "Hey, Leila. What do you think of this Wookiee sound?"

I put on Jed's headphones, which were tight and sweaty, and a wild growl assaulted my skull. The effect didn't sound un-Wookiee-like, but it was rather wetter than I would have expected. "Wow," I said. "What is that?"

"I ate an entire Meat Lover's pizza and recorded myself vomiting into the toilet. What you're hearing is actually that sound played backwards. I wanted something really guttural, you know?"

"Well, it's definitely guttural. Maybe add a little . . . reverb?"

"Yeah. Reverb. Cool. Reverb."

I left Jed muttering and returned to my station. I liked him. Jed had idolized George Lucas his whole life, and in his mind, copying Lucas would make him just as good as Lucas. I didn't think that was how it worked, but I admired the strategy nonetheless. Plus, it was always nice to spend a little time around a total weirdo. It helped keep my own life in perspective.

The other thing I liked about Jed was that he knew about my drug problem and he didn't give a shit. When we were the only two people in the room, I would snort up my powders right in front of him, and he did me the kindness of not even acknowledging it. We'd edit together until the sun rose outside our windowless South LA haven, and the regular people with their unfathomable normal hours started to show up. I liked Jed just about the best of anyone I'd met at school.

That night, the two other kids in the room eventually shut down their computers and left for their beds. My drugs came out. I'd locked the picture on my Mamet thing but didn't feel like going home yet. Jed was still there at his station, staring and clicking and nodding away. I watched him and snorted a bump off the edge of my car key.

"Hey, Jed?" I said.

Jed took off his headphones and swiveled his chair around to face me.

"Are you a virgin?"

I didn't ask it to be mean—I was just curious, and Jed didn't take offense, just like I knew he wouldn't.

"Yeah," he said without shyness. "I got close once, with this pretty Leia from a convention, but that was a couple years ago."

I nodded and examined his expression, but I couldn't read it. I was in the mood for a cigarette. Instead, I asked, "Would you like to not be a virgin?"

It didn't take long at all, and I didn't even bother locking the door. Once we were finished, I kissed Jed on the top of his head and gathered up my stuff. He sat there very still, with that same undecipherable expression on his face, until he finally smiled at me. It was a very gentle grin and, again, not at all shy. I smirked back and did that thing where you separate your fingers V-like.

"Live long and prosper," he said. "That's *Star Trek*, though."

"Oops." I shrugged and headed out.

• • •

The next day, I found myself staring at the mural that covered the handball court outside North Valley Middle School. A multiracial family held hands in front of a boxy house with a smoking chimney and a white picket fence. Above the house, a rainbow and a sun did their damnedest to invalidate all the lessons in proportion being taught on the other side of the high wall. The rainbow had only four colors, and the sun wore sunglasses—I couldn't decide if that showed that the sun was overconfident or had low self-esteem. That was the question that plagued me as I waited for Jordan, my smart and charismatic new Adderall dealer, who happened to be twelve years old.

Jordan was late, and I was impatient. He was a child actor I became acquainted with at a classmate's barbecue, and the star of *DracuLia*, a hip and modern retelling of the Dracula story that airs on ABC Family. He played Lia's half-vampire little brother, cursed with the catchphrase "Anyone want to fang out after school?" Jordan ran a hell of an impressive drug ring, selling off the overflow from the prescriptions of dozens of his hyperactive preteen buddies. He might have been a budding criminal mastermind, but at the moment he was just late.

I checked my phone. There was a text from Mari asking me to pick up more rattraps and a missed call from my mother I wouldn't be returning anytime soon. But nothing from Jordan. I settled on the idea that the sun can be arrogant and insecure at the same time.

Finally, Jordan rounded the corner on his skateboard, wearing a Dodgers cap and bright-white sneakers. He nearly crashed into me before hopping off his board and giving me a big hug. "Sorry," he said. "Math test."

"How'd you do?"

"I think you mean how did Micah Goldberg, who sits in front of me, do?"

I shook my head and thought about telling the kid not to cheat.

Jordan looked around and pulled a stuffed animal from his backpack. The cloth monkey's stomach had been hollowed out, and my drugs were nestled inside.

"What's this one's name?" I asked.

"Skeeter. My cousin won him shooting guns at a fair."

I put Skeeter in my purse. I could never bring myself to throw these stuffed animals away, so my bedroom had become a graveyard to Jordan's childhood. I handed the kid a book, *Huckleberry Finn* this time. A wad of cash was taped to page sixty-seven.

"Finished with *On the Road* yet?" I asked.

"Yeah, I read it in, like, two days. It was awesome."

"You a Sal Paradise man or a Dean Moriarty man?"

"Dean, obviously. He's the one with the real balls. I want to take a trip like that when I turn sixteen."

I smiled.

"Oh, hey, Leila—bad news. The Becker twins, these eighth graders who have thirty-mil scripts, got shipped off to some program for fuck-ups in Arizona. So I might be a little short next week."

"Okay, pal," I said, though my brain was thinking, *Shit, shit, shit.*

I wanted to tell the kid to study for his math tests, to stop dealing drugs, and, no matter what, to never, ever start taking them.

But Jordan probably already did tons of drugs, and he probably already had straight A's—it takes one to know one, after all. He was surely going to get into a great college and continue his career as a cute kid actor. And who was I to offer advice to anyone? It was eighty-five degrees out, and I was wearing leather. I felt chilly, yet sweat clung to my back like toxic seawater inside a wet suit. So instead of saying anything, I started to walk away. In my head, I was already inside my Prius, crushing up pills atop my Tom Waits CD case and inhaling a way through the rest of the day.

"Hey, Leila," Jordan said when I was halfway down the block. I turned back around. "Do you want to go to the spring formal with me?"

I grinned and gave the kid a little salute.

"It's during lunch."

In my head, the drugs were already inside my body, and I was working harder and harder until I couldn't feel anything at all.

"See you next time," I said.

Chapter Twelve

I was in my second year of college when I met Harlan Brooks, the man who remains to this day my fair-weather agent. He called me up out of the blue one afternoon, saying he'd heard about this whiz-kid writer with a pen like Sam Shepard's and a body like Samantha Mathis's. And he wanted to know if I'd join him for dinner. I almost hung up, but I thought it might be my dealer, Angus, playing a dumb joke, and I'd been having trouble tracking him down.

"Angus?" I asked.

"Who? No, this is Harlan Brooks, calling you from my sunny corner office on La Cienega—"

"Come on, idiot, you haven't seen the sun in a decade—"

"Hey, take it easy. I'm calling to tell you that I think you're the next big thing and—"

"Seriously, Angus, would you knock it off?"

Harlan took a breath. "Look, Leila, I think we may have gotten off on the wrong foot. I shouldn't have said that thing about Samantha Mathis. It's an outdated reference for one. Someone like Rachel Bilson is probably a better choice. Anyway, I'm trying to tell you that I've been following your work for a few years—I'm kind of a theater buff, really.

I mean, I played Tevye in high school. Anyway, I'd like to take you to dinner to talk about what I think you and I can do together. Does that sound like something you can work with?"

I paused and asked weakly, "Are you sure you're not Angus?"

Harlan just laughed and hung up.

I called my dealer to confirm that he was, in fact, a separate human, and when he picked up, I went over there. Angus was a seventh-year senior at UCLA who still lived in the dorms with his ferret, Angus. His door was double-padlocked from the inside, and when he opened it slightly to appraise me, I looked straight into a pair of wild, bloodshot eyes.

"Where have you been? I've been trying to get ahold of you for days."

Angus let me into his room, and I sat down on a pile of books that had served as a makeshift chair for as long as I'd been coming here.

"You know that actress I told you about? Freshman who started here this year? I can't say her name, but . . ." Angus winked and pointed to a signed poster above his desk. Teen actress and legendary former baby-pageant champion Jolee Jessup smiled at me from the center of a pink heart.

"She had some big bender at her new house in Malibu. Called me over, and invited me to stay too."

"Wow. Was it enlightening? Have you renounced your scholarly ways to join a pop band?"

"Why do you always have to be so cynical, Leila?" Angus was cutting lines with a razor blade atop a copy of *A People's History*. He shook his head. "Man, those Disney girls can get *fucked-up*."

"It's in their DNA. Ten years ago, it was another pack of fruit snacks to get through the audition."

Angus inhaled a line. "Hollywood, yo."

"Hollywood, yo."

As I drove home with a bottle of Adderall and a just-in-case eight ball tucked into my purse, I thought about that bizarre call from

Harlan Brooks. By the time I reached my apartment, the drugs I'd done at Angus's were starting to make my nerve endings feel like they were being fucked by a group of lovesick teenagers—which is to say, I felt fantastic. So I picked up my phone and dialed the last number that had come in; sure enough, an agency assistant was on the other end. She connected me to Harlan, who answered with a "Lay it on me, babe. You in for dinner?"

"Yep, I guess I'm in for dinner."

I met Harlan at Beast, a trendy restaurant on Highland with a meat-only menu. I spotted him at a table in the front, a thirty-five-ish short guy in rectangular glasses and an expensive purple tie. When he saw me walking toward him in the drapey cream-colored minidress I'd thrown on before leaving the house, he yelled across the room, "You're not a fucking vegetarian, are you?"

In response, I ordered the crispy pig's head in pickled vegetable aioli with a side of veal's tongue—kind of disgusting, but I was trying to make a point. Over dinner, Harlan laid out his plan for our beautiful future together. He would introduce me to the world as a hotshot "it girl" right away—before I even had to do anything—and we'd sell lovely little screenplays together for all eternity. I'd be in magazine spreads and on marquees, and we'd both be rich. "All you have to do is trust me," he said. "And try a bit of this shallot-crusted steak."

When Harlan got up from the table for the third time and returned with an extreme case of the coke sniffles, I knew we'd get along just fine. And that sentiment was toasted over half a dozen drinks at a little dive bar across the street called The Nickel. The bartender was a world-weary Irish lass named Angie who kept sighing like she wanted to cut us off—except for the fact that neither of us was having any trouble holding our liquor. I imagine the cocaine helped with that.

After he took yet another trip to the bathroom, I asked Harlan if he cared to share what he was holding. He looked me over with a wry little smile plastered across his tight, pearly mouth. "Hey, Leila, I know I just called you a wise old screenwriting sage, but you're still a kid."

"Sounds like you're just being greedy," I replied.

Harlan insisted on coming with me while I snorted up his powder, to make sure my heart didn't explode right then and there in that bar on Highland—for that would be the glamorous whiz-kid story without the payoff. So we locked ourselves in the unisex bathroom to the chagrin of the fiery waitress. "Nothing unsavory, Angie," Harlan yelled.

Inside the small bathroom, Harlan pulled out a vial of white powder, and I took a mirror from my bag. I tapped out some of the blow and snorted it with a rolled-up Post-it, my instrument of choice. (There are germs on dollar bills, and germs can kill you!) I did one line, then two lines, then three lines, while Harlan watched. "Well, bravo then, you little psychopath," he said. "You're even more ready for this lifestyle than I thought."

I flipped him off with both hands and left the bathroom. I ordered another round from Angie, and a scotch and soda was waiting for Harlan when he returned. We bullshitted for a while about movies, realizing we found all the same things funny and all the same things boring. And then he tried to get down to business. "So," he said. "Here's the thing about Los Angeles."

"I *know* the thing about Los Angeles, dude."

He continued. "It's all facade, of course. That great big shiny sun we worship so fervently has been bedazzled, and those nighttime stars were commissioned by Swarovski. But everyone here thinks they're a *part* of that facade. So all you have to do is convince them that they're right, make them feel like you're going to help them live out their fantasy, and in return, they'll help you live out yours. Even when there's no money, there's money everywhere. You just have to know whose vase to overturn."

"I mean, I already have a plan," I said.

"Do you now?"

"Yep. You want to hear it?"

"Lay it on me."

I stood up and tapped my nose. I walked back to the bathroom and left the door open. Harlan came in and started cutting lines. We took turns snorting, one after another, and I could feel my head filling up like a snow globe. I was dizzy and entirely too high, close to a breaking point.

"And . . ." Harlan said. "Your big plan?"

I steadied myself on Harlan's shoulder and waited for the snowflakes to part. I fought the rush of blood flooding my head, leaned forward, and whispered into his ear.

CHAPTER THIRTEEN

I told Harlan I was on board to work with him, and he immediately started sending me out on meetings with creative executives and their associates, executive creatives. The first job I secured was a pilot for ABC. The studio wanted "a hip and modern retelling of Robin Hood as a teenage girl." It took a bit of work, but Harlan finally convinced them that I was just the gal for the job, what with my insight into the hearts and minds and hormones of the youth and all.

I was used to a heavy pace of academia, so I handled my classes at USC without much trouble. Not that this was any great accomplishment. One such class was called Creativity Seminar—the professor would bring in broken headlights and old shoes and other artifacts of shit, and we were supposed to let ourselves be inspired by the ugly mundanity of daily life (not a problem for me). My more challenging and, dare I say, more legitimate courses were handled with my tried-and-true writing-everything-on-Adderall process. Add my natural distaste for sleep, and I had more than enough time to dedicate to the Robin Hood project.

Nevertheless, in terms of research, I did none. Mari and I watched *Men in Tights* one night because it happened to be on, but that was the extent of it. Instead, I reached inward, pulling out truth and beauty from the well of wisdom located inside my own body, somewhere around the pancreas. I decided to set the thing in an upper-crust Los Angeles private school called Sherwood (there's an actual upper-crust Los Angeles private school called Oakwood; feel free to gasp over my brilliance at any point). My Robin Hood was Rocio, an East LA girl from a poor family who attended the joint on scholarship. She was a total badass and, naturally, totally hot. In the pilot, Rocio develops a flirtatiously antagonistic relationship with a handsome lacrosse player whose father happens to be on the school's board of trustees. She fucks him and robs Pops blind, but then gets all guilty about it after she realizes she has real feelings for the kid. Especially after he turns up in East LA for the block party Rocio organized with the stolen money.

Here are the notes I got back from the studio:

- *Confused about the name Rocio. Like that she's ethnic, but we don't want her to be so ethnic that she alienates the audience.*
- *Sex in the pilot??? Should wrestle with losing her virginity as a season arc.*
- *Can we add a mariachi band to the block party?*
- *Board of trustees should mirror bad guys in orig. Robin Hood. Same names, etc.*
- *Wasn't there also a priest character in orig. story? Can we add a priest?*
- *Like gay brother character. Could be more flamboyant. Could add stuff with priest.*
- *Do we have a role for Betty White?*

At the end of it all, the show didn't get picked up, thanks to news of a "a hip and modern retelling of 'Little Red Riding Hood' as a teenage *boy*" over at FOX, but the studio was happy enough with my work that a steady stream of it started coming my way. There was another pilot, then a few rewrites of ABC Family movies and some TV stuff.

Nothing huge, but solid work that a lot of people in this town would kill for.

My favorite job was a freelance episode I wrote for an hour-long ABC drama called *Grace's Hope*. The show centered on the daughter of a conservative church family that had been uprooted from a small Southern town and dropped inside the bowels of New York City. In my episode, Grace is offered, and consents to smoke, that demon, marijuana, for the first time. Never one to avoid being a pain in the ass, I made up my own pot lingo and assured the studio it was real. In my script, a joint was a "tapeworm"; a bong, a "periscope"; and the munchies became the "diabetes jones."

The show flew me out to New York the week my episode shot. I had a midterm for my evening class on Alfred Hitchcock to take the night before, so I finished the script quickly, drove to the airport, and dashed onto a red-eye. As soon as I landed at JFK, I hopped in a cab, threw my bags down at the Ace Hotel, and caught another taxi over to the set in Brooklyn. Call time was 8 a.m., and I arrived only half an hour late, a personal record. I poured myself some coffee at the craft services table, headed directly for the chair labeled "Writer," and fell immediately to sleep.

The actress who played sixteen-year-old Grace was actually a twenty-three-year-old stick of dynamite named Melanie. She smoked cigarettes between takes, wrapped up in a fringed suede jacket, then slipped seamlessly back into the skin of the pretty blonde innocent she'd been hired to play. I noticed that Melanie was staring at me as I came to from my little nap. As soon as I'd cleared the fog from my brain enough to participate in eye contact, Melanie winked and raised her eyebrows mischievously. At lunch, she cornered me by the condiments. "Okay, be honest: 'tapeworm' I can believe, but 'periscope'? There's no way anyone calls a bong that."

"Sure," I replied. "Those are all real terms, straight from the marijuana community of the greater Los Angeles area."

"Bullshit," Melanie said, and put her hand on her hip.

"All right, yeah, it's bullshit. I made it up."

"You're a fucking psycho." Melanie laughed. "I love it. There's a party tonight at the Chelsea. You're coming with me, and if you even try to argue, I'll hand your lying ass right over to the producers."

For the rest of the afternoon, I was kept awake by my writerly duties. The director called me over to do a few line rewrites for the scene where Grace confesses to her father that the oregano in the little baggie on her desk is, in fact, not oregano at all, but rather an eighth of "Lucifer's sage." They wanted me to add a tearful hug and a bit of praying, during which they'd voice over a message from Grace's cool new dealer friend.

After shooting wrapped for the day, Melanie headed to the wardrobe trailer and clothed herself in a blue minidress and studded heels. She fastened her long blonde hair into a fauxhawk and painted herself with eyeliner. Over the dress went that fringed jacket, which I now noticed was embellished with two small buttons, featuring Joan Jett and Dusty Springfield. Melanie offered me a dress, but after I'd spent two straight days inside my leather leggings, the pants had become like a second skin I was afraid to shed, lest my skinny bones and sinewy muscles be revealed raw under the lights of New York City.

To say that I was underdressed for the party would be an understatement, as it would be to call it a party. Properly, the event was a "salon," meaning we were all there to edify one another over cocktails via incendiary conversation—or, if worse came to worst, a game of Balderdash. The apartment belonged to a rich kid named Lindsey Valmont, who split his time between a suite of rooms at the Chelsea Hotel and a loft in Williamsburg. Evidently, he was some kind of critic whose actual credentials no one could seem to track down. Lindsey greeted me and Melanie at the door in a checked bow tie, his expensive hair coiffed high above a pair of John Lennon glasses. Inside the apartment were various twenty- and thirtysomethings dressed in gowns and suits, sipping wine and champagne out of crystal. A Leonard Cohen record played on the stereo, and the wall opposite the front door was decorated with a large print of Robert Mapplethorpe calla lilies. "Welcome to my not-so-humble abode," Lindsey said, kissing Melanie on the cheek and then on the neck.

"Lindsey, this is Leila. She's writing my show this week."

"A friend of Mel's is a guest of mine," Lindsey said, pecking at my face before I had a chance to duck out of the way.

Lindsey brought us drinks, and Melanie and I made our way over to the couch, where two couples were discussing a fiction piece in the *Paris Review*—some story about a troubled young woman who inherits an old parakeet from her eccentric great-aunt.

"It was very Lorrie Moore," one of the women said. "But also kind of Alice Munro."

"I couldn't help but think Joan Didion," the other gal chimed in.

"And of course there was *so much* Virginia Woolf in the semicolons."

"I read it on the shitter," a man in a pink sport coat said. "Which gave the writing a not-unwelcome scatological undercurrent."

"Hmm," I said, raising my eyebrows thoughtfully. "Didn't you find the parakeet to be a little caricaturish?"

The man pondered this, and the women nodded and murmured.

"You know, now that you mention it, I actually did," Pink Coat said, turning to address me head-on. "And did *you* feel that the dialogue was kind of derivative of *Gilmore Girls*?"

"I don't know," I said, shrugging. "I haven't read the story."

Melanie cackled out loud at this and grabbed my hand, leading me away from the stunned group of aesthetes and over to an open window, where she placed cigarettes in our mouths. "These people are fucking idiots, aren't they?" Mel asked.

"I wouldn't argue with the description."

"What are we doing here?"

"Hey, these are your friends, lady."

"Nah," Mel said, sparking her Gauloises. "I don't have any friends. These are just people who want to say that they know me and people it makes sense for me to know. Or some shit like that."

"Don't get all sentimental on me." I laughed.

Melanie took my hand and played with the ring on my index finger. "Thanks for coming with me," she said. "I'm glad I don't have to sit through this on my own."

I smiled at Melanie, feeling a little overwhelmed by the sudden attachment this girl I'd met only twelve hours earlier had clearly formed, and not entirely sure where it was heading. I pulled my hand away and tossed my cigarette out the window to land in a puddle or a gutter six stories below. I glanced around the room. Lindsey was roaming about with a fistful of assorted pills, instructing his guests to close their eyes and pick one at random. I could see Percocet in there and Valium and maybe ecstasy. I guessed there were probably some uppers as well, but Lindsey caught me trying to peek and waggled his finger in the way only a man in a bow tie can. Then he walked directly to where I was perched on the arm of one of his overstuffed white chairs and held out his palm. I closed my eyes, selected a smooth round pill, and swallowed it down. "Take another," Lindsey said, and I did.

By the time midnight rolled around, I was feeling mercury-mouthed and a little dizzy. The room had begun to take on the characteristics of a biology experiment: people shifted and moved at a variety of paces; discussions turned into monologues, and monologues into hysterical laughter. Lindsey turned off the Leonard Cohen and cleared his throat to prime himself for an announcement. "I've got something really special in store for you guys tonight," he said, gesturing to a small, pretty Korean woman standing at his side. "Helen here is a pianist who's just graduated from Juilliard—and lucky us, she's agreed to give a little concert."

Helen seated herself at the grand piano in the center of the room and banged out something complicated with a hell of a lot more notes than seemed necessary to my deliriously high ears. After two songs, I began to get restless, so I quietly slipped out the front door. I wandered into the hall, gripping the gold railing along the staircase, feeling disoriented as I stumbled through the holy hotel. I sat down on a step across from a gray-toned Joan Miró painting. I stared at the surrealist blobs hanging crookedly on the wall, suspended in a series of rows, and tried to figure out what in the fucking fuck kind of drugs I was on.

I don't know how long I'd been zoning out on the painting when I registered footsteps behind me. I turned to see Melanie hovering over me, her long legs made infinite by the angle. I smiled up at her, and she tilted her beautiful blonde head over the railing. "Listen," she said. "I think you're sexy. I mean, I think I have a crush on you."

"How's that concerto going?" I asked, beckoning Melanie to come join me on my step.

"Yeah, I can't go back in there. Jesus Christ, I mean, who stops a party for a goddamn piano recital?"

"Once again, Miss Melanie, they're your 'friends.'"

"Ugh. Let's get a room, yeah? Just to hang out and maybe nap?"

"Sure." I smiled at Melanie and ran my fingers along the brown fringes of her jacket.

Melanie went down to the concierge and booked us a room on the fifth floor. We walked into the small white space, and Mel slammed her back up against the door. "Jesus Christ, I am so fucking high," she said. "You want another cigarette?"

"Sure."

Melanie and I crawled through the window and out onto a small fire escape, letting our feet dangle over the edge of the railing. My head was spinning, and the horns and catcalls from the street below blended into some harmonious thing that sounded more to me like music than any of Helen's living-room gesticulations. "I like New York," I murmured to Melanie, and then cracked up over my grandiosity.

"Do you?" Mel asked. "I'm not sure I'm sold on it."

"How come?"

"I dunno. I'm from a small town, and I miss it. I was in LA for a little bit, and then I was gonna move to Peru. My girlfriend's there. She's a photojournalist, doing a book on the indigenous tribes of South

America. But I landed the role of Gracie, so I guess I have to call this place home."

"You don't have a home. This is just a place that wants to know you, and a place it makes sense for you to say you know."

"I'm too high to tell if that's the most profound thing I've ever heard or the stupidest."

"Absolutely the latter."

"Yeah." Melanie made circles with her dangling feet. Her right shoe flew off and went tumbling downward, where it landed in a puddle. "Oops."

A cab rolled over the shoe and flattened it. We both winced at the same time, like the car had smashed our bodies instead.

"Okay, so you dig New York," Mel said. "How do you feel about LA?"

"Hard to say. It's the only place I know. I mean, at this point, I don't think I could even leave it. And try something else. Is that sad?"

Melanie kicked off her other shoe, and we both breathed a sigh of relief when it landed softly on a bag of trash. "The world is big."

"Too big."

"Enormous." She shut her eyes and curled her bare feet beneath her. "I think I prefer it small."

Suddenly dizzy again, I put my head on Mel's shoulder. I could feel her heartbeat pounding against me, so brave and so sweet. I brushed up against the soft skin of her neck. I let my eyelashes flutter out a Morse code message my brain and mouth were too destroyed to convey, and it made perfect sense. She kissed me gently. We let the horn music wash over us as our lips found some sort of rhythm outside of place and time and ingested substance.

We floated in from the fire escape and landed on the bed, where we strung ourselves out like a tangled-up set of Christmas lights. Melanie's hands were inside my shirt, and my thigh was up against the small of her back. Skin fused with skin, and hair tangled with hair. Mel moved down the bed and pulled off my leather pants—that safety blanket

I had been fearful of shedding all day—but it all suddenly felt okay. There was white powder in the air, and I had no bones, so I couldn't be scared. Melanie put her head between my legs, and I reached my hand out to touch a scar along the side of her torso. But before I got there, my head clouded, my body was vibrating, and I was just plain gone.

• • •

The next morning was hell. Melanie and I both woke up late, hungover, to a barrage of angry voice mails. I felt like death, but Mel was much sicker than I was. We hailed a cab and stopped on the way to the set so she could buy a cheap pair of flats. All day, Mel kept taking breaks to vomit in her trailer while I held back her hair and the fringe of her suede jacket. I was at the craft services table, alternating sips of coffee with sips of water, when I felt a tap on my shoulder.

"Leila?"

I turned but couldn't quite place the young face I was looking into.

"It's Jordan."

"Oh my God." It was, in fact, Jordan, my formerly twelve-year-old Adderall dealer who was now fully into the early stages of puberty. Makeup covered a few splotches on his face, and his hair was tousled through with at least three kinds of product. "What are you doing here?"

"I'm in the episode. I play Prince Henry Saint Xavier. I saw your name on the script and wanted to text, but I lost all my old numbers."

"Well, you look *exactly* like I pictured Prince Henry. But now I feel bad that I gave your character a pot scene."

"I think I can handle it." Jordan smiled. His white teeth and arched eyebrows telegraphed pure confidence. "We're shooting that later, actually. I love your weed slang. Even though it's totally fake."

"Shhh." I winked. "Don't tell."

"All your secrets are safe with me." He winked back, and I was suddenly blindsided by a deep and choking fear—but for which of us, I wasn't sure. I took a sip of coffee and a sip of water.

"You look tired," Jordan said.

"Jet lag."

"I wish I could help. But you know, I'm not really doing that anymore."

"No, that's okay. That's good." I nodded aggressively. "I should really go lie down. But hey, it was great to see you, kiddo."

"Wait." Jordan reached out and touched my arm with unexpected shyness. "I brought you something."

He held out a book. It was Mark Twain's *A Double Barrelled Detective Story*.

I took the book and looked it over.

"It's empty," Jordan said. "Just, you know, pages and stuff."

"I love it."

"I don't know if you've read it, but it's a lesser-known one. I figured, since you're the one who got me into Twain and all."

"Thanks, Jordan." I took the book, and a second later, my eyes were wet. "I'll read it on the plane home."

I smiled at the little prince and walked back toward Mel's trailer. I put the book down on the counter and quickly forgot all about it. Back in Los Angeles, I realized what I'd done and promised myself I'd buy another copy—for my own sake, not his. Jordan was going to be just fine. And I was oddly relieved when I realized it had been me I'd felt scared for.

CHAPTER FOURTEEN

After I turned in my next project, a modern retelling of *The Emperor's New Clothes* featuring the emperor as a hot teen girl, Harlan goaded me into joining him on a trip to Vegas, along with some of his agency buddies and their clients. It seems he'd become concerned by my behavior. I was showing up to all my meetings late—but still turning all my projects in on time, I always made sure to note—and he decided all would be fixed if I just took a few days off. We flew out to Nevada on some producer's private jet. I ordered a Bloody Mary and kept my sunglasses on because everything felt too bright.

One of the clients along for the ride was a handsome writer from New York named Ellington, a scowly guy who appeared generally miserable in a fun sort of way. He kept an unlit Marlboro Red in his mouth and had chocolate-brown eyes that seemed distantly amused. After fifteen minutes of flirty glances, I killed my Ray-Bans, hopped out of my seat, and slithered up beside him.

"So," I said, crunching the ice in my Bloody Mary. "How does a white fella like yourself come to be named Ellington? Parents musicians or just fans?"

"My old man's a critic. Jazz guy for the *Village Voice*. He thought Miles was too prosaic."

"And Thelonious was too poetic."

Ellington chewed his cigarette. "Leila Massey. I know about you, right? You're, like, twelve years old, but you already have more credits than half the town."

"Thirteen, and I've hardly even gotten anything made."

Ellington cackled. "Yeah, well, if getting stuff made was the marker of success in Hollywood, everyone in here would be on a public bus instead of a private jet."

"What about you? Ever have anything up on the screen to show old Jazz Pop?"

"Couple things. Indie feature that did pretty well at Sundance. A parable-type story that used vampires as a metaphor for zombies."

"Sounds zeitgeisty," I said, and Ellington snarled.

The plane was landing in Vegas, so I returned to my seat for the descent and ordered another Bloody Mary. Harlan, sitting in the row in front of me, turned around and looked directly into my eyes. Sans sunglasses, they were the color of my beverage. "Jesus Christ," he muttered, and handed me a bottle of Visine.

As the only woman on the trip, I got my own private suite at the hotel. I took a shower and blow-dried my hair. I jumped into a slinky emerald dress, boosted my system with amphetamines, and left to meet the guys down at the hotel bar. Ellington had spruced up a bit himself. He wore a gray blazer over his plaid shirt, dark corduroy pants, and blue Jack Purcells. The Marlboro in his mouth was lit this time, and he was playing he-loves-me-he-loves-me-not with shots of bourbon and a glass of IPA.

"Hey, Leila," Harlan said, interrupting the penetrating once-over I was giving Ellington. "What are you drinking?"

"Bulleit, please."

One of the other agents, a dimpled dipshit named Brandt, turned his chair so it was facing me. "So we've been talking, and we've decided you need to take acting lessons."

I looked at Harlan. "Oh yeah?"

"Yeah. We think you should be writing stuff for yourself to star in. That's how you're going to build a real empire. We want to put a pretty face to all those pretty words."

I shrugged. "I don't know, guys. I'm not sure I have it in me to be one of *those people.*"

Ellington turned from his spot at the bar and addressed the row of agents. "Jesus, you're seriously encouraging someone to become an actress? Here's the one woman in Hollywood who actually doesn't want to be on camera, and you're trying to change her mind? You should be showering Leila with prizes, not pleading for her to take up the profession."

Brandt looked at me. "Ellington can't stand LA. He thinks it pales in comparison to his precious New York City. He despises all of us vapid assholes and dearly misses the company of real intellectuals and avant-garde assholes."

"Fuck you, Brandt." And with that, Ellington was up and out the door. I downed my drink and followed him. Harlan yelled after me, but I didn't turn around. I could feel my agent fighting the urge to run over and plead with me to have another drink and maybe book a massage and a facial instead of following the surly writer with the Marlboro Reds down whatever path it might take me.

I found Ellington in front of the elevators, pacing back and forth. He lit another cigarette. "That guy's a prick," I said.

"Everyone's a prick," Ellington replied. "I fucking hate Vegas."

"Amen to that. You ever been to Joshua Tree?"

. . .

We rented a car and got halfway to our destination before we pulled over and made out furiously in the backseat. Once in town, we checked in to the cheapest, shittiest motel in the area—the furthest thing from our first-rate Vegas digs. And so Ellington and I found ourselves housed inside the yellow-and-brown walls of the San Bernardino County Inn and Out—lying naked on a bed with a busted spring, idly watching a spider work its way across the ceiling, and wondering what in the hell we should do next. For Ellington, that ended up being heroin.

"Look, I'm not a drug addict or anything," Ellington explained, placing a baggie of yellowish powder on the rickety bedside table. "But when I do partake, heroin is my narcotic of choice."

"You don't have to explain yourself to me."

"It's just that, seeing as this is a vacation and all, I'm going to be ingesting some of this."

"Yes, I got that."

"You're welcome to join me."

I watched him carefully tap out a bit of powder and cut slender lines—these servings were much more svelte than the mounds of cocaine I was used to inhaling. It was the first time I'd ever seen heroin live and up close, and the hue was what I'd describe first and foremost as "sickly." Still, I was tempted. And more than that, I was curious.

Since Ellington was only a casual junkie, he sent the drugs racing through his nose without hitching them a ride on the back of a needle. He inhaled a single line, and I witnessed the exact moment the opiates hit his bloodstream. He appeared to be in pain—his eyes clamped shut, and his jaw dropped open. But of course, he wasn't in pain at all; he was in ecstasy.

"What does it feel like?" I asked.

"Fucking . . . good."

"Use your damn words."

"Um . . . it's warm. Warmer than warm. Like tiny individual blankets have been knit for each one of my cells. Like . . . you know . . ."

Ellington drifted off before he could finish his explanation. But it didn't matter, because I knew I wanted what he was offering. I craved tiny cell-blankets, warming up my neurons and soothing my blood. I would kill to drift off in ecstasy, to lose my mind for an hour or two. I looked at the remaining lines of heroin sitting right there on the table and thought about how easy it would be to lean over and snort one up. How nice it would be to give my brain a break.

But I didn't do it. I wasn't quite there yet. The time would come when the sickly pale yellow of powdered heroin would be as familiar to me as the sickly pale yellow of the back of my hand, but it wasn't going to be here inside this hotel room. Not just yet.

CHAPTER FIFTEEN

I soon dropped unceremoniously out of USC, leaving for winter break and just never going back. I was writing instead of attending class anyway, and I figured I'd gotten about as much out of the place by then as I ever would. Harlan had consistently landed me jobs doing adaptations and rewrites for teen-focused projects, and he figured it was time for me to start taking on bigger, more name-making scripts.

He called me up one day. "I'm sending you an article. It's about a cult leader, man named Marshall Viner. Guy herded all these teenage runaways out to his ranch in Central California in the seventies, and half of them were never heard from again."

"Sounds up my alley."

"Tell me what you'd think about doing an adaptation. The studio just attached an actor, and they're looking for fresh blood to hammer out a script. I think I can get this for you."

"Who's the actor?"

"Guy named Johnny Isherwood. You know who that is?"

My heart skipped a beat. I knew who he was, all right—in fact, I knew more about Johnny Isherwood than I could admit to without suffering grave embarrassment. Dark-haired, green-eyed, and slightly snaggletoothed, Johnny had started his career as a teenage model in NYC. He was soon bitten by the acting bug and starred as Prior Walter in a revival production of *Angels in America*. Rumor had it, he was bitten by the heroin bug not long after that. Nevertheless, Johnny was quickly snapped up for an HBO ensemble drama about the world of professional ballet, and he simultaneously booked half a dozen leading roles in indie features. He was right on the precipice of superstardom, and the cult movie could be a breakthrough gig for both of us.

Harlan worked his magic, and I landed the job. However, the producers constantly reiterated what a risk they were taking by entrusting the project to my delicate little lady hands, and Harlan was forced to vow fervently on my behalf that I wouldn't let them down—which meant I'd actually have to do some research. But first, I was going to meet with Johnny.

"You're good to do this, right?" Harlan asked me one evening over breakfast. "I mean, you have your shit together these days, yes?"

"Of course," I said, and halfway meant it. "Everything is totally under control."

Johnny wanted to convene on the Universal lot. He passed along his cell number and told me to text him when I arrived. He didn't respond to any of my inquiries as to where, exactly, on the Universal lot he felt like meeting, so I parked my car somewhere central and typed out a missive. *Where to? Commissary? Office bldg? Men's rm glory hole?*

Johnny sent back a building address and told me to wait outside. I walked to the spot and fussed with my hair. I checked my eye makeup and smoothed my tank top over and over until I could see the silk starting to fade. After ten minutes, a golf cart came zooming around the corner, pushing every bit of its half-a-horse-power. Johnny was smoking a cigarette in the driver's seat. He wore a plain black shirt and his hair, shaved on the sides, was slicked into a pompadour. If Ellington had been a four or a five on the scale of junkie mystique, Johnny was a full-on ten.

"You the writer?" Johnny asked, his head slowly rolling around to look at me.

I nodded.

"Well? Hop in," he said, barely giving me time to scramble into the passenger seat before revving up that pathetic little engine and zooming off.

"I'm Leila," I said, and Johnny just nodded.

We drove in silence for a minute. "Where are we going?" I asked.

"You ever done the Universal tour?"

"As a kid I think, yeah. Whoopi Goldberg narrates it or something?"

"Fuck if I know," Johnny said as the cart zoomed onto the backlot. The front part of the Universal lot was all office buildings and soundstages while the back section contained old sets—some of which were still being used for production. Johnny drove us through a Western ghost town that radiated emptiness, and brown paint peeling under the flat North Hollywood sun.

"Are you shooting something here on the lot?" I asked.

Johnny ignored my question and began to narrate like a tour guide. "This here is Old Western Town. Which was used in that great movie *The Sheriff of Old Western Town*."

He zipped the cart past a saloon and a county jail, and around to an enormous water pit. "If you look to your left, you'll see the pool that was used in that famous diving sequence in *The Graduate*. Which is a completely overrated movie."

"Blasphemy!" I cleared my throat and lowered my voice. "Although it looks far too large to be a regular swimming pool, such a set was necessary to keep Dustin Hoffman's nose in perspective."

Johnny cracked the barest trace of a smile and kept driving. Eventually, we rounded the corner toward the Bates Motel, the legendary building from Alfred Hitchcock's *Psycho*. Here, Johnny idled the golf cart. He lit another cigarette and glanced up the hill.

"Should we get out," I started, "or . . . ?"

Johnny blew a smoke ring. A minute later, one of the big blue tourist trams began driving up the hill. As it crept up to the set, the door of the Bates Motel suddenly swung open and a man—Norman Bates himself—walked out wielding a giant knife. He stalked toward the tram, and a couple of tourists shrieked. But just in time, the tram started up again and continued driving up the hill. Norman put down his knife and walked casually back into the motel.

I laughed. "That's great."

Johnny didn't say anything; he just cut the engine and stepped out. I stayed in the cart, unsure what the plan might be. He walked up to the door of the Bates Motel and knocked. Norman poked his head out, and, seeing Johnny, opened up. Johnny turned to me. "You coming?"

There was very little inside the room, and certainly nothing that might peg it as the interior of a motel. A few chairs, a desk, and a mini fridge were positioned around the room, all pretty dusty. Books and magazines were scattered everywhere, and a laptop was open to a PDF of a script.

As soon as we were inside the room, Johnny disappeared into the bathroom. I smiled tentatively at Norman Bates, who stuck out his hand. "Yo, I'm Bradley."

"Leila," I said. "So how do you know Johnny?"

"We were roommates when he first moved to LA."

"Oh, cool."

"Not really. It was a shithole on Franklin."

"Well, it sounds less murdery than the Bates Motel."

Bradley grinned. He was tall and good-looking despite his pasty pallor—a pretty fair approximation of Anthony Perkins, even up close. He offered me a chair. A moment later, Johnny came out of the bathroom looking a little dazed, but also content. He'd run water over his face, and some of it had pooled around the collar of his T-shirt. I watched him cross the room, unable to stop my eyes from flying over his arms in search of track marks. "So," Johnny said, sitting down on the floor across from me and really looking at my face for the first time. "Let's meet. What's up with this project?"

"Well, I'm still in the preliminary stages of the script. Just doing research first, you know? There's a book by one of the women who escaped from Marshall Viner's ranch, and I'm reading that."

Johnny nodded and tapped his fingers against the side of his leg.

"And there's another book," I said, suddenly feeling shy and unprepared. "Sort of an unofficial biography of Viner. It's pretty interesting, and, um . . ." I smiled nervously. "Would you excuse me? For one second."

I got up from the chair and walked into the bathroom, where I rolled my eyes at my own reflection in the cracked mirror. I ran the tap and pulled some powder from my bag. I dumped all of it out onto a makeup compact and pushed it into two enormous lines.

"Focus," I whispered to myself before I snorted up the drugs. I flushed the toilet for show, and by the time I had reached my seat across from Johnny again, I could feel my brain grinding itself into a sharp point.

"So," I said, talking quickly and finally feeling in control. "I've got those books, which are great, but I'm also doing some ground research. There's some kind of commune situation out in the desert I've been hearing about. Lots of lost little rich kids giving everything up for a life of caves and free love. Kind of like a permanent Coachella, I guess."

"Huh," Johnny laughed. "Bizarre."

"Totally. I guess it's getting popular, but there's basically no information about it on the Internet. Definitely sounds like a culty affair to me."

"When are you going?"

"Leaving tomorrow," I said. "Hey, you should come."

I regretted the overeager invitation instantly and tried to backtrack. "For character research, I mean. But I can just as easily take notes for you. Or maybe you've already got your own thing going on—"

"Sure," Johnny said, shrugging.

"Wait. Really?"

"Why not? But I get to drive, cool?"

I nodded, not letting myself believe that I was actually about to take a trip to the desert with Johnny Isherwood. There was just no way something like that could happen. We talked about the movie for a while longer, pausing to watch Bradley intermittently grab his prop knife and become Norman Bates. Later, Johnny drove us back down the hill in the dark, nearly crashing the cart into a tree. He stopped at the lot where my car was parked, and idled the engine. He smiled at me, a grin that was at once relaxed and full of mischief.

"Well," I said, getting out of the cart. "I'll see you tomorrow?"

"Yes, ma'am," Johnny said. There was a flash of motion as he grabbed my wrist. He pulled it so I tumbled back toward him. Then he grabbed my head and kissed me, deeply, but only for a moment.

Johnny turned his head back toward the road and revved the engine. I stumbled out of the cart and walked through the parking lot, trying hard not to smile. I had just kissed the matinee idol of my goddamn dreams, and tomorrow he was loading up his needles, picking me up, and driving us out to the California desert.

PART TWO

Cactus Needles

CHAPTER SIXTEEN

EXT. FERRIS WHEEL — MORNING

A Ferris wheel stands alone in the middle of the desert. It rotates through the air. Down below is a camp: there are tents, double-wide trailers, a makeshift stage, and rocks painted with Navajo patterns in neon colors.

Leila and JOHNNY sleep in one of the Ferris wheel's carts. As the ride reaches its apex, Leila wakes up. She tries to stand but is very wobbly. She looks around, confused.

Below is a SKINNY GIRL who wears a bright-pink feather headdress.

                    LEILA
              (groaning)
        Oh. My. God.

Suddenly, Leila leans over the edge. She vomits, spewing bile inches from the girl's feet.

The girl looks at the ground and then up at the Ferris wheel. Absurdly, she just grins.

                    LEILA
          What the fuck?

Johnny starts to laugh from his place on the floor of the cart. He doesn't even open his eyes.

                    LEILA
          Ugh, why are you laughing?

Leila slides back down to the floor.

                    LEILA
          And how the hell did we even get
          here?

Leila rests her head on Johnny's shoulder.

                    JOHNNY
          Five more minutes. And then we'll
          get up.

Johnny's hands napped on top of the steering wheel—pale digits with dirty fingernails and small black stains—so immobile they barely balanced the burning cigarette that was in the process of stinking up our shitty little car. I studied the maddening stillness of Johnny's hands with bouncing eyeballs and wondered which of us was in better shape for driving. We were heading east on the I-10, etching a path through the methane-gas wasteland that sits outside Los Angeles. Big rigs rolled along to our right, and elderly pickups sputtered behind us. Ahead, an impoverished pasture steamed under a flat bed of light.

We had the radio tuned to a country-pop station for the exciting reason that it was the only thing Johnny's duct-taped antenna would pick up out here in suntanned cow land. Soft-voiced and sleepy-eyed, Johnny intermittently crooned original lyrics over the twangy guitars. "I like deep-fried Jesus and shootin' guns. I'm the boy next door, and I'm on the run."

"Didn't we just hear this song?" I asked.

"I got a woman loves her daddy and braised Christ. She's got a head full of maggots and a heart full of lice."

"I swear, this was on ten minutes ago. Your lyrics took a weird turn."

Johnny smiled at me. "Me and my woman gonna have some motherfucking fun. I'm the boy next door, and I'm on the run."

"Hey, Johnny?" I said, smiling despite myself and trying in vain to find another station. "You are anything but next-door."

Johnny took his hands off the wheel. The car helped itself to two lanes as it barreled forward on the smooth concrete. I spun around toward Johnny right as he leaned over, grabbed me by the head, and kissed me hard. He returned his grip to the steering wheel just in time to veer us out of the path of a big green Heineken delivery truck. The truck's horn blared behind us for the next mile, competing with the radio static that burst in through the speakers.

"You are a fucking lunatic," I said, shaking my head and leaning over to light us a pair of cigarettes.

Noon had long come and gone by the time Johnny picked me up from my apartment in Silver Lake. Although we'd only been driving for a few hours, the sun was already descending into a hazy blue lighting setup. We rolled along in silence for a while. I stared into the infinite absolutely-fucking-nothing out the window and tried to block the dark thoughts that were creeping their way up from the recesses of my muted brain. That's what quiet does to me. I noticed that Johnny had begun to squirm in his seat, and I could feel myself coming down from the wad of amphetamines I'd ingested before leaving the house. It didn't make me sick, per se—the aches and gut-fire and cold sweats came much later—but even en route to the dwelling of an underground cult, with a movie star seated inches to my left, being drugless made me feel completely and utterly normal. And that's what I'd learned to hate the most.

"Hey—you want to be on the lookout for a rest stop?" I asked Johnny, throwing my hair up into a ponytail to prevent it from crawling along the back of my neck.

"Yeah," he said too quickly. "I have to, uh—"

"Yeah, I do too . . ."

We followed a "Food/Gas" sign off the freeway and parked the car. Johnny and I walked to the bungalow of bathrooms and split up according to the pair of stick figures who silently announced implications about our respective genitalia. Inside the filthy restroom, I splashed cold water on my sticky face, reapplied the eyeliner that had smudged to raccoon-mug proportions, and prepared myself for the rush of synthetic energy that was headed my way.

I realized with annoyance that most of my drugs were stashed in the duffel bag I had hastily packed and thrown into the trunk of the car, and I didn't feel like waiting for Johnny to finish his own clandestine fix. I held the remaining bit of what was once a gram of cocaine up to the fluorescent lightbulb, tapped the sides free of clinging powder, and rummaged around in my purse until I found a renegade Adderall hiding amongst a pile of copper Lincolns—an orange thirty-milligrammer, perfect for cutting into quarters. I crushed it, mixed it in with my coke, and snorted the whole thing up with two Olympian inhalations.

The sun had almost set by the time I finished freshening inside the bathroom. I wandered into the convenience store and bought a bottle of water and a pack of cigarettes. The carcinogen-baked old man behind the counter looked me over, eyeing judgment onto my leather shorts and studded ankle boots. "I seen you and your feller pull in," he said.

"Oh yeah?"

"You two's headed out to that New Age commune, ain't you?"

"You know about that?"

"Sure I do. Young folks like you are always stopping in here all eager-beaver and loading up on energy drinks." The man slid my purchases toward me. "Never see any of 'em on the way back out, though."

I put the cigarettes in my purse and walked outside, locating the spot where Johnny was leaned up against a gas pump, slowly rocking back and forth. I slid in front of him and looped his arms around my waist. He rested his chin on top of my head and ran his hand across my stomach, tracing his high onto the flesh underneath my gauzy tank top. He dug his fingernails in and exhaled.

"How you feeling?" I asked.

"Goddamn fantastic," Johnny replied.

"Well then, I guess I'd better drive."

Back in the car, I raced above the speed limit as nighttime opened up around us. The sky turned black and became speckled with stars. I looked at it and tried to see something other than residue on a glossy coffee table after all the cocaine has been snorted up. Johnny stuck his head through the window and smelled whatever was out there. "You want to hear about the first time I saw stars?"

"Mm-hmm," I said. "As long as you don't turn it into a country song."

EXT. FERRIS WHEEL — MORNING

Leila removes her head from Johnny's shoulder. They're
rotating slowly through the air. The Ferris wheel
creaks and moans like a demonic basset hound.

> LEILA
> Should we get up now?

Johnny murmurs. Opens his eyes and looks out over the
edge of the cart. Young people walk around in various
states of undress, high-fiving each other and cooking
breakfast.

> JOHNNY
> How about just one more time
> around?

> LEILA
> Yeah. Or two.

On the floor we see a burned spoon and strips of bloody
cotton.

The glowing Ferris wheel was the first thing Johnny and I had seen for miles that wasn't a cactus or a menacing rock formation lurking in silence up against the horizon. It was the dead of night by the time we pulled up to the rickety wooden base that, even with the machine turned off, seemed to struggle under the weight of all those metal carts. Taking in the half-built structures and signs of fresh hooliganism, we figured this must be the camp we were looking for. We were surprised by all the quiet, however; we had expected a perpetual party fueled by glow sticks and pills and various other up-all-night synthetics.

We parked our car off to the side of the main road and walked back to the camp through the dusty silence of the desert. Something howled off in the distance, and I shivered despite myself. Johnny laughed. "You spooked?"

"I didn't expect it to be so damn quiet," I said. "I don't do very well with quiet."

Johnny put his thin arm over my shoulder and pulled me toward him. The creature howled with double vigor. "Girlie, whatever's out there is more afraid of you than you are of it."

"That's bullshit. For all we know, that could be some teenage were-wolf, driven to bloodlust by raging hormones and Red Bull."

"And for all the werewolf knows, we could have shotguns."

"Why didn't we bring shotguns?"

Johnny and I entered the camp quietly, stepping over empty whis-key bottles, bicycles, and discarded articles of clothing. All the various living structures—tents, makeshift shacks, a few trailers—were set up in a large circle. One enormous and roughly crafted picnic table sat in the middle of it all, flanked by two long benches hand-painted in Day-Glo colors. An empty pizza box from God-knows-what-kind of delivery system was being licked over by a small white cat, and half-full bottles of wine idled on the table. Still, there wasn't a single sign of waking human life. It was as if the whole camp had been beamed away into outer space by a gang of aliens with a raging case of the munchies.

Johnny pulled the little cat off the pizza box and held it in his hands. He seemed as baffled as I was by the emptiness. "This is definitely the right place?"

"Neon tents, fixed-gear bikes, skateboards . . ."

"Okay, okay."

"Unless we stumbled into the aftermath of an Urban Outfitters catalog shoot, I imagine this is the only spot of its kind out here in Desert Nowhere."

"Well, maybe that howling werewolf ate everyone up."

"See any duct tape around?" I turned toward Johnny and raised the most menacing fist I could muster. "Or am I going to have to sew your mouth shut with cactus pricks?"

Johnny grabbed me by the arm and spun me in a circle. I looked into his green eyes, which shined like a "go" signal in the moonlight, feeling the desert rolling around me. I leaned forward and shoved my tongue down Johnny's throat. He put his hands around my hips and squeezed downward, like he wanted to hold the entirety of me between two fingers.

Still carrying the little cat, Johnny walked over to the table and picked up one of the labelless bottles of blood-red merlot. He sniffed it and grabbed another. He handed me one of the bottles and held his own up in a toast. "To a pair of functioning drug addicts, alone in the middle of Bizarro Siberia."

Johnny's sudden honesty after a car ride full of avoidance and innuendo took me aback. My first instinct was to deny, to get indignant and claim I didn't know what he was talking about. In my head, I ran through a list of excuses: all the work I had to do, the pressure, the timetables, the "what business is it of yours, anyway." I thought of accusations I could throw back his way: at least I wasn't shooting the family-size pack of heroin every day and hiding my arms under jackets in the dead of summer. But what would the point of that be? I was a drug addict, and lying about it would just make me seem all the more desperate.

So I clinked bottles with Johnny and took a long, messy swill of wine. "Is it that obvious?" I asked.

Johnny just laughed. I took the white cat from him and rubbed it behind the ears. "How long have you been shooting dope?"

"A while. Long enough that I don't remember what I'm like without it."

"And you're just honest about it?"

"No," Johnny said, shrugging. "Not really."

"Yeah," I said, and closed my eyes. There was too much goddamn quiet everywhere, and it was driving me crazy. "Where the fuck are we?"

Johnny wanted to commandeer a tent and pass out for the night, but I figured it would come as an unwelcome surprise if the kids returned to find us huddled up in one of their houses—and we needed them to like us. We talked about sleeping in the car, if only to experience life as sardines doused in tobacco. Rejecting that, I pointed to the Ferris wheel.

"It's practically a boutique hotel," Johnny said, and climbed into one of the carts. He reached his arm down, and I handed him the cat. Then he pulled me up. I unrolled my jacket and set it out on the bench. Something else howled in the distance: a different, angrier-sounding thing. I was wired and on edge from these unfamiliar desert sounds. If the noises around me had been coming from an ambient sleep machine, I would have hurled the thing at the wall, stepped on it with a booted foot, and put on *Sticky Fingers* instead.

Johnny settled onto the bench and opened the small tan backpack he'd kept close to his side all day. He pulled out his rig and spoon and looked at me carefully. "Do you mind if I do this here? I can go somewhere else if it bugs you."

I shook my head and took out my ponytail. "You don't care if I watch?"

"Nah, if it's okay with you."

I nodded and popped gum into my mouth to murder the acidic taste of the long day. Johnny undid his belt and wrapped it around his bicep. He carefully measured water and tapped a chunk of brown tar into his spoon, heating it all with a lighter. He let the mixture absorb into a cotton ball and sucked it up into his syringe. Then he shot himself in the arm.

Johnny inhaled suddenly and leaned back. I couldn't take my eyes off him. He opened his mouth as if paused in oration and gasped with his whole body. Then a sleepy smile spread across his face, and he became very still. The desert cracked. Something scurried on the ground beneath us. I swooped around to get a look at it but saw only shadows. I shivered against the pounding of my heart, wanting to leap up and walk around, but physical activity of any sort seemed the furthest thing from Johnny's rapturing mind.

So I stuck out my arm. "What do you say? Can I have some of that?"

Johnny sat still for a moment, considering. Trying to be human. "You ever done this before?"

"No," I said. "But I hear people like it."

Johnny laughed. "People tend to."

My arm shook a little.

"Are you sure? This really isn't something to fuck around with."

"I know," I said, and looked him dead in the eyes. We both held the stare.

"Okay then."

Johnny pulled a fresh needle from his bag and asked me to hand him a cigarette. He ripped out the filter and unrolled it until it was just a small cotton ball. He tied his belt around my arm and repeated his process of mixing and heating.

I took a deep breath.

He kissed my vein. I shut my eyes.

Johnny plunged the needle in, pulled it back to siphon up my blood, and, just like that, released a sucker punch of heroin into my body.

Fuck, fuck, fuck, holy fuck. I fell backward. I leaned forward. My body was somewhere else. I saw the desert sky come closer, I heard the hum of another world, and I felt bunnies, soft sand-colored bunnies, crawling all over me.

EXT. FERRIS WHEEL — MORNING

As their cart reaches its lowest point, Leila and
Johnny jump out. A cloud of dust forms as they land,
stumbling to the ground. They gather themselves.

                    VOICE
          Whoa, whoa, whoa!

Leila turns and sees a LONG-HAIRED KID running toward
them. He is shirtless and holds a piece of wood.

                    KID
          Are you guys okay?

                    LEILA
          Yeah, I think so. Johnny, you
          alive?

                    JOHNNY
          All good. Just a little dusty.

The kid looks around.

                    KID
          Where did you two even come from?

                    JOHNNY
                (deadpan)
          Hollywood.

They laugh. The kid shrugs and returns to whittling his
piece of wood.

EXT. CAMP — CONTINUOUS

Leila and Johnny take in the scene as they head toward
the camp. Kids in their late teens and early twenties
walk around. A NAKED GIRL is lathering herself with
a bar of soap as her friend shoots her with a Super
Soaker.

Leila glances down at her leather shorts.

                    LEILA
          Why do I suddenly feel overdressed
          for the occasion?

With sunglasses shielding our eyes from daylight's fiery breath, Johnny and I walked through the camp, getting our bearings. Two dozen tan slips of kids in bikini tops and bright tees strolled around. None of them looked older than twenty-five, and most appeared barely a pimple to the other side of teenage. A young guy in a striped tank top and cheap neon glasses waved me over. "What's up? You look new. Just get here?"

"We drove up last night. It seemed like no one was around, though?"

"Yeah, we all went out to the caves to take peyote and try and talk to Gram Parsons."

"Did you reach him?"

"Nah, but our DJ was playing some righteous shit. If he's out here, he definitely heard us."

"I'm Leila." I stuck out my hand to shake.

"Rex."

I turned to point out Johnny, who was standing a few feet back, smoking a cigarette. A trio of girls were ducked down behind a trash can, staring at him and giggling.

"You heard of that band Sitting Bull?" Rex asked.

My answer was a no, but I nodded anyway. "Yeah, I think so."

"They're coming up to play tonight. I'm stage-managing."

"Awesome. We'll check it out. So, um, is there someone in charge here?"

"Yep. That would be Kennedy. He's out at the moonshine distillery, but if you're around later, I'll introduce you. Kennedy and I went to high school together. I've known him forever."

I nodded. "That would be perfect."

I collected Johnny, and we went in search of shade and a place to sit down. "That was Rex," I said. "He believes in ghosts and has shitty taste in music. I feel like I'm going to puke again."

I ducked back behind a small succulent and vomited up what had to have been the last remaining bits of my stomach. I pulled the bottle of water from my bag and rinsed out my mouth. I felt dizzy and exhausted. Johnny kept lighting cigarettes and squinting off into the distance, like he was waiting for a cowboy gang to ride into town on the backs of chestnut stallions. "Motherfucker," he said. "I could use some coffee."

I rummaged around in my purse and pulled out a box of caffeine pills. I popped a couple out and handed two to Johnny. He swallowed them dry. I took mine with water and threw in an Adderall. The fact that neither Johnny nor I had eaten anything in the last twenty-four hours crossed my mind, as a fact but not as a craving. Truth be told, the only thing my body felt like putting inside of it was more of that sorcerous brown tar. But I fought, or maybe ran from, the urge like it was a stranger in a dark alley. For I was an addict without a doubt—pills and white powders filled my days and nights; amphetamines had so formed my identity that I wasn't even recognizable without them—but I sure as hell wasn't a junkie.

EXT. DESERT — DAY

Leila wanders around with her cell phone, trying to find
service. She does and sees a message: 15 MISSED CALLS.

She presses "Play" on one of them.

                        MARI
                   (via voice mail)
          Hey, chica. It's Mari. Where the
          fuck did you go? Are you still in
          the desert with that hot actor?
          Have you boned him yet? Fucking fill
          me in already. Jesus. By the way,
          your agent came by looking for you.
          I kinda stalled. Said I hadn't been
          home much. But he seemed upset. Are
          you in trouble with him? Oh yeah--
          and I found rat shit in the silver-
          ware drawer, so I threw the whole
          thing out. Looks like we're a plas-
          tic-fork household from now on--not
          that you ever eat anything anyway.

CHAPTER SEVENTEEN

Kennedy reached onto a shelf—a ledge in a rock, actually—and pulled down a mason jar full to the brim with clear liquid. He unscrewed the lid and handed it to me. "Bananas, pears, and acai," he said as I took a swill of the potent moonshine. "It'll fuck you up and shoot you full of antioxidants at the same time."

Kennedy was dressed almost entirely in leather and suede. He had a fringed poncho on over his bare chest, raw denim jeans, and a pair of tan motorcycle boots. His brown hair hit his shoulders in a wavy cascade. His eyes were golden brown and intense, and they smiled at me while his lips tucked over the corners of his own mason jar. I swallowed a cautious gulp of the alcoholic concoction. It was strong and sweet, like some sort of postapocalyptic nectar served only at the finest nuclear-bunker speakeasy in town. "Wow," I said, letting the potent sip crawl around my insides. "That's strong."

"Not bad, right?" Kennedy asked.

"Pretty good. Do you guys sell this stuff?"

"Nah. It's just our way of being self-sustaining, you know?"

"Living off the land. All those local acai plants."

Kennedy winked at me with one of his amber eyes. As if to make a point, he pulled a bag of mushrooms from his pocket and offered me a stem, which I accepted but didn't eat.

Kennedy had made his home inside a giant cave that he'd converted into a dwelling as covetable and cool as any *Vice* magazine spread. A lofted bedroom jutted out over the kitchen and living area. The space made use of natural ridges in the rock to provide a lopsided array of built-in furniture and storage room for stuff like books, records, and seemingly untouched cookware. What wasn't provided by nature's Pottery Barn, Kennedy had crafted to fit perfectly within the confines of his modernist cave. He offered me a seat on a driftwood-and-sheepskin couch. I cozied up to a crocheted throw pillow while Kennedy scooted his stool right across from me and hunched forward. "So," he said, scorching my retinas with eye contact. "What is it that you would like to know about me?"

I had skirted the issue of why, exactly, I was here, striking the word "cult" from my vocabulary and instead emphasizing the film's focus on "avant-garde lifestyles." Kennedy seemed receptive to letting me and Johnny talk to him, but he wanted us to do it separately. Given Johnny's natural inclination to not give a shit about anything, at all, ever, I was up first.

As I struggled to find my way into easy conversation, Kennedy glanced at my hand, which was still holding on to that psychedelic mushroom stem as if it were the string of a long-deflated balloon. He held up a finger and meandered over to his kitchen area, returning with a jar of honey and two spoons. He popped a mushroom of his own into his mouth, chewed, then chased it with a spoonful of the sticky substance. He stared into my eyes, clearly waiting for me to follow him inside whatever dripping lava lamp of a world he was headed off to. Resisting my natural aversion to psychedelics (fuck dreamlands—I have a hard enough time simply falling asleep), I gave in and swallowed the bitter mound of dried fungus, saying a silent prayer to fortify my stomach against anything too warm or fuzzy. I ate a spoonful of the honey and then another, once I realized it would be the only foodstuff to hit my digestive system in quite some time.

"Well?" Kennedy asked again. "Do you want to know my favorite color? What living or dead celebrity I'd most like to have dinner with?"

"Neon isn't a color," I shot back, eliciting a grin inside those golden eyes. "Why don't you just talk to me about what you're trying to accomplish out here."

I knew it wouldn't be that simple, but I had to give it a shot anyway. I had tried to gather some sort of a mission statement from the kids at the camp, but no one could come up with anything more substantial than babble about rejecting mainstream society and building something better, and "Have you heard the new track from DJ Robot Horse?" They all seemed to worship Kennedy, but in this abstract way that didn't line up with an actual person. They spouted the party line of "being a part of something" but had a hard time offering any insight into what that something might be. What I was curious about was Kennedy's own level of awareness—whether he was manipulating the kids into following along in his little experiment in hipster exile, or if he actually bought into this idea that something important was happening out here.

"Are you having a good time with us?" Kennedy asked.

"I am," I said, answering in earnest.

"Is there anything you're missing?"

I shook my head. "Not really."

"Well, what you're experiencing is pretty much what I'm trying to accomplish. We're having fun, and no one's getting hurt. And if we can all become a little less reliant on the bullshit trappings of society in the process, then even better."

Kennedy opened up a tin of Nat Sherman cigarettes, black with gold leaf around the filter. I wanted to ask him how much they cost. And for that matter, I wanted to know how much money it took to bring indie bands out into the middle of the desert twice a week. I was curious exactly how many thousands upon thousands of dollars were sitting inside a trust fund with his name engraved on the outside. I guess given our rapport so far, I could have just come out with all that, but I didn't. And I'm pretty sure that was because I didn't want any conflict to get in the way of the fun.

So instead, I flashed a smile and took the cigarette that was offered to me. "Good times aside, we can both agree that the DJ who sampled the *Doogie Howser* theme kind of sucked, right?"

Kennedy laughed. "Just wait for the next band. They'll be up later this week, and they'll blow your mind."

"Let me guess—there are three ukuleles?"

That was the last question I asked that made any sense. As if cued up by some hidden party producer, the ridges in the rocks started to vibrate, and I felt the warm desert air enter my lungs with a burst of clarity. The crocheted throw pillow in my lap became as interesting as a Pollock painting, and I found myself hopelessly lost—without map, compass, or Magellan GPS—inside Kennedy's golden eyes. I suddenly wondered if Gram Parsons might be hanging around, after all.

Kennedy and I spent the next few hours lying around in his cave, watching stuff crawl along the outside of our eyeballs, and laughing at nothing at all. A small lizard wandered in from outside, and we gave him a name and a backstory. Little Ajax had just reached the age of maturity and was on a walkabout to find himself before he could reenter the suburban lizard society from whence he came. I picked him up and let him spend some time crawling along my arm, but eventually my attention fell to other things (you ever notice how truly fascinating split ends can be?), and Kennedy and I lost track of our little reptilian friend.

When the effects of the mushrooms were starting to wear off, Kennedy pulled a vial of cocaine from his pocket and dumped some out onto a small mirror. "Time for an afternoon pick-me-up."

I licked my lips. Seeing my eyes spark with light, Kennedy laughed. "I guess I should have known this was more your speed."

"Pun intended?" I asked, as I leaned over to snort up a line.

"But of course."

• • •

After my meeting with Kennedy—which ended with the camp's leader walking me through the grounds with his arm thrown around my shoulders, introducing me as "the Lizard Queen"—the rest of the kids embraced me and Johnny as members of their ilk. They knew about our motivation for being there, the movie we'd come to research, but that didn't make them wary of us; it just made them feel like they were going to be famous. Johnny and I decided to hang around for a little while longer, so we rented an Airstream trailer owned by a guy named Lennox who had skipped off to Amsterdam to track down the perfect lady of the night and bring her back as his wife.

Johnny and I would sleep through the sunny parts of the day and emerge a little before dusk, like a pair of go-getter vampires. We spent our nights guzzling lavender wine with the kids—getting high to celebrate the execution of every bottle—and stumbling into cacti like Buster Keaton in Roy Rogers drag. Embracing my role as the Lizard Queen, I'd pull Johnny up to the tallest point of a series of rock formations. From that angle, we could see the camp only in the periphery, and the rest of our field of vision was occupied by a flat vista of stars that seemed to stretch on forever.

One night, as a DJ played ambient electronica for the coyotes, Johnny and I collected a group of kids to join us at our usual spot. These youngsters were on all sorts of shit at once—pot, peyote, the ancient piss fumes of vintage denim. It was as if all their boundless freedom had turned their drinking and drugging into a facsimile of revelry. The kids were strangely methodical in their need to keep on going. The music never got turned down, and the bottles of wine and jars of moonshine kept appearing—these kids were not going to be caught unprepared for the eventual climax of whatever Kennedy had in store.

Amidst the drinking, a tiny blonde was trying her damnedest to get Johnny to dance with her. I nudged him until he gave in and conceded to sashay around with the girl, who wouldn't stop babbling on about how her grandmother used to take her to the ballet in London every year. Evidently, Grandma had box seats. Apparently, the ballet is a place where one can have box seats.

After a do-si-*do*-not-fucking-make-me-do-this-again, Johnny snuck off to fix, and the girl sat down next to me. She looked incredibly bored yet was trying incredibly hard to appear both interesting and interested in everything. It was a point on the spectrum of facial expressions I hadn't even seen before, a gaze so unreachable I felt a stab of pity in my blackened heart. "Is he your boyfriend?" the girl asked, looping a series of tiny braids into her blonde hair.

I smiled and avoided the question. The girl continued to play with her tresses.

"So, how long have you been out here?" I asked, remembering my supposed reason for staying at the camp.

"About six months," the girl, Zoemarie, replied. "I met Kennedy at a party and then just skipped out on my last year at Wellesley. He's so brilliant, you know? Like, I knew I just had to be a part of it."

"A part of what?"

"Um, this."

"And what, exactly, is this?"

Zoemarie just stared at me, like I was a mongrel in need of a safety helmet and a diaper. Johnny returned before the girl had a chance to wipe drool from my chin and send me back to Silver Lake on a converted short bus. He kissed me casually on the top of the head. Zoemarie shifted her attention back to her hair, using individual braids as the strands to make bigger braids, and turning herself into a pint-sized Medusa with a head of Ouroboroses.

Johnny pulled me up from the rock, and we walked back to our trailer arm in arm. My lanky companion swayed a little as he moved, and I was feeling drunk enough that the amphetamines in my system were dulled to half capacity. They were rocket ships that were fired off at light speed but then boomeranged right back, disappointing a room of NASA astrophysicists, who had been hoping for infinity and beyond.

Inside the trailer, Johnny kissed me softly for a long time. His eyes were becoming half-lidded. He fell onto the bed, and I helped take off his jeans, running a finger along his sharp hip bones. He smiled dreamily. "How long do you want to stay?" he asked, in a way that made me think it wouldn't make a difference to him if my answer were for one more day or one more year.

"Play it by ear?" I said as I slipped out of my clothes and into one of Johnny's T-shirts. The blanket we were using was a bright, coarse tapestry that made me feel like we were dust mites living beneath a floor mat—an apt metaphor if I'd ever heard one. I climbed under the covering and pulled it up around Johnny. He draped his leg over mine. His hand meandered under my shirt and softly caressed me all the way up my torso before coming to rest atop my collarbone.

I turned to kiss him, but he was out cold. So I flipped back around to face the other direction and counted sheep. When I ran out of those, I counted alpacas, and llamas, and then I counted little faux Indians beneath a cocaine sky.

• • •

The next morning was really the next afternoon, and once again, my head felt like it was being attacked by an ogre wielding a dull hammer. I wrapped myself in a flannel shirt and headed outside. In a corner of the camp was a small generator, and attached to that was a series of extension cords, one of which fed life into a black plug that trailed up to a Keurig individual-cup coffeemaker. I'd discovered the machine my second week in the desert, and instantly all that outdoors became a little more homey. I'd been making trips to visit the appliance every afternoon and evening, throwing a couple of dollars into the box of coffee canisters to help with whatever magical system these folks had for getting their provisions out to the desert.

On the first day of the coffee, I managed to track down a pair of Styrofoam cups, riddled with teeth marks and starting to corrode, and

I'd been rinsing them out for reuse since. I filled each with dark roasted liquid, took a long, heavenly pull from one of the cups, and wandered out to deliver the other to Johnny, who was sure to be in need of this particular kind of afternoon fix. Johnny wasn't in the trailer or hiding from the sun in any of his usual places, so I sat down at the big table in the middle of the camp to wait for him to reappear. I pulled out my notebook and jotted down a few of my recent thoughts and impressions. (*Dear Diary, the desert's weird! It's both hot and cold!*) The notes I'd taken since coming to the camp were rather underwhelming, and the feeling that I needed to delve a bit further into this whole research thing was beginning to gnaw at me like it was the jackrabbit I secretly feared would find his way to that precious Keurig extension cord.

I heard a trio of high-pitched giggles coming from a nearby tent. Acting on a pretty plausible hunch, I walked over and peered through the gauzy curtains. Sure enough, Johnny was inside. He was reclining in a chair while a young girl shaved his face with a straight razor. Another barely legal wisp was cleaning his boots with wax and a cloth while a third hovered around simply tittering at everything Johnny said. I stood at the entrance for long enough that I couldn't just slip away, and the group took notice of me.

"Leila, hey," Johnny said, beckoning me inside. The girls looked at me nervously and faded into the background.

"Brought you coffee," I said, stepping through the curtains and handing Johnny his cup from an arm's length.

"Thanks, kiddo," he said, grinning in that lazy way of his. His green eyes were calm and soft and unconcerned. I guess another word for that is "high."

"Sure," was all I replied.

Every once in a while, I'll get a jolt of something nonsynthetic and very raw running through my body, which reminds me I'm still something of a human being. I guess this is what's referred to as "emotional pain" by the normal, nonvampiric person. Watching those girls flit around Johnny, I suddenly realized that for all our ostensible coupling, he and I hadn't even slept together. One of us was always too fucked-up to make something as insignificant as having sex a priority; our romantic overtures were tiny gestures offered in between a sniff and a shot, a cough and a nod.

Johnny took a sip of his coffee. "What are you up to?" he asked, running a finger against his freshly shaved chin, which still had dollops of Barbasol all over it.

I suddenly felt the need to crawl even deeper into the invisible shell I'd built up around myself, out of sarcasm and quips and a little bit of Bubble Wrap. "I don't know," I said, pretending nonchalance. "I guess I should try to get some work done. That is why we're here, after all."

I felt a couple of bubbles in my protective shell pop.

"Cool," Johnny said, sounding totally unfazed as the skinny barberess wiped shaving cream from his face with a wet towel. "See you around dinnertime?"

"Yeah, maybe."

I turned and bolted through the front curtain. I reached into my pocket and fingered an Adderall, sending it on an express ride through my digestive system via a gulp of coffee. Outside in the flat desert air, I tossed my notebook from one hand to the other, my mind a vibrating muddle of stuff I didn't want to think about. I swilled the rest of my coffee, crumbled the Styrofoam cup, and made my way to Kennedy's cave.

Kennedy was sitting outside on a stool with a stoned fella in shorts and white boat shoes, testing high-end headphones. With a giant noise-canceling pair plugged into an iPod, Kennedy was nodding his head in approval. When he saw me coming, he sent the guy on some errand and beckoned me inside. I took my seat on the driftwood couch and Kennedy fetched me another jar of that antioxidizing moonshine. "Back for more interrogation?"

"Yeah," I said, my leg tapping violently against the side of the couch. "I guess I need to hound you until more of my research is done."

We sat in silence for a moment.

"I don't think that's why you're here," Kennedy eventually said, fixing his amber eyes on my irises. He didn't blink, and I looked in vain for evidence of a bug or a fossil buried inside. "I think you're here because you want something from me."

"Sure," I said. "I want to talk to you about my project some more."

"Nah." Kennedy crossed one foot over the other. "You're upset about something, and you think being around me will fix it."

I scoffed and shook my head, alarmed.

"So. Do you feel better?" Kennedy asked.

"No," I said. But I did.

And there it is, I realized, biting my tongue to keep myself from shouting at Kennedy. *The key to my story.* I had it figured out, the reason two dozen kids had followed this long-haired twentysomething away from the comfort of their parental-funded apartments and VIP after-parties, past outlet malls and casinos, and straight into this land of dust and cacti. It wasn't that Kennedy had some unique vision or special insight into our souls; it was that everything he said was issued without fear of consequence, and every action he took was done without any sense that the principle of remorse even exists. The confidence, the lack of second-guessing, was utterly irresistible—and I found myself wanting to ask Kennedy to explain my own life to me. In other words, what I'd learned is that everyone loves a sociopath.

The instant my mind latched on to this idea, I had to test it. I had to see if Kennedy was really so blasé and indifferent to consequence. And for that, I had to make him lose control. The two of us sat in silence, our conversation now a staring contest. His eyes burned into my own, and the words "Do something unexpected" ran through my head. Without looking away, I settled on my default method for trying to gain the power in a situation: I took off my shirt.

Kennedy didn't flinch, nor did he smile. I unlatched my bra and dropped it on the ground. Kennedy cracked his jaw and continued looking directly into my eyes. I got up. I walked over to the hand-crafted armchair Kennedy was so arrogantly sitting in with his legs

spread akimbo and his hands folded behind his head. I glanced over to
the sheets that served as a front door and made sure they were pulled
shut. I got down on my knees. I looked into Kennedy's eyes, but there
was no new reaction at all, just that same honeyed glow that radiated
a bemused impenetrability. It was like he could care less where I went
with this thing. I was losing the contest, but I couldn't stop. I undid
Kennedy's belt and opened the buttons of his dark blue jeans, and tried
to swallow a way out of my own head.

CHAPTER EIGHTEEN

INT. AIRSTREAM TRAILER - DAY

Leila inhales a line of Adderall.

The place is a total mess. Leila's sitting on the floor
with her notebooks spread out in front of her.

> LEILA
> (to herself)
> Okay, idiot. You are going to write
> now. Today is the day you get some-
> thing done. You're not going to be
> useless anymore. No way, nohow.

She snorts another line.

> LEILA
> That was a terrible pep talk.

Leila flips through her notes. She shakes her head.

ANGLE ON: A note that just reads "Keurig Coffeemaker!"

She flips to another page.

> LEILA
> (reading)
> "His eyes had a honeyed glow that radiated a bemused impenetrability?" What am I supposed to do with that?

She snorts another line. Looks around. She gets up and starts cleaning the trailer, folding shirts and gathering discarded underwear.

She brings a black T-shirt over to Johnny's bag. A little black toiletry case falls out. Leila opens it, and inside are a needle and a wad of black tar heroin.

Leila sits back down. She gets up. She walks over to the drugs and hovers.

> LEILA
> Fuck it.

Leila goes to the cabinet and pulls out a spoon. She winds a belt around her arm. She unravels a cigarette and pulls out the cotton filter.

She pours water into the spoon and adds some heroin. She heats the mixture and sucks it up into the needle. She tries to find a vein but misses.

                         LEILA
          Damn it!

She tries again. Nothing.

                         LEILA
          Come on, come on.

One more time. It hits.

                         LEILA
          Oh!

Leila's eyes glaze over, and she slowly slumps backward
onto the floor.

SMASH CUT TO:

EXT. FIELD — DAY

A family reunion in the enormous backyard of a country
home. Two dozen adults and children hover around picnic
tables.

LITTLE LEILA (5) sits on a swing, pumping back and
forth. She zooms through the air and giggles.

ANGLE ON: A younger JIM and BETH, who watch their
daughter on the swing.

                         BETH
          Does that look sturdy enough to
          you?

Leila waves.

> LITTLE LEILA
> I want to go higher!

The swing set starts to creak and groan.

> BETH
> (yelling out)
> Leila, be careful!

> LITTLE LEILA
> Higher, higher, higher!

> BETH
> Jim, do something. She's going to
> get hurt.

> JIM
> It'll hold. She needs to learn her
> limits.

Beth grimaces. Leila laughs wildly as she continues to
pump.

> LEILA
> Higher, higher!

Suddenly, the swing gives one big creak and snaps. We
hear joyous, maniacal laughter, and then we see black.

Chapter Nineteen

"Jesus Christ!"

Johnny's voice jolted me awake, alarming me with its volume.

"Fucking goddamn it, what the fuck!"

Normally soft and tempered, his words felt like they were assaulting me from the inside of my own skull.

"Please . . . just come on."

The first thing I felt was cold, and then wet, and then really, really confused. I was confused as to why I was on my back being pelted with icicles as they broke through the holes of the showerhead. Confused as to why I was wearing all my clothes. Confused as to why I was so fucking confused. The mummified expression on Johnny's face didn't provide any answers; he managed to look both completely terrified and utterly zoned-out at the same time.

"What's going on?" I asked.

Johnny leaned over and touched my face. "Oh my God, you're alive."

I coughed.

"I fucking thought . . . Jesus."

I coughed and coughed. Johnny turned off the shower, and I shook the water off my face.

"Hi."

"Are you okay? Do you feel okay?" Johnny held my hands in his own.

"I'm wet," I said. "And cold. What are we doing?"

"You fucking OD'd."

"What?"

"I came in, and you were lying on the floor, turning blue."

I took notice of the invisible anvil that was crushing my head against an invisible boulder.

"Christ, I thought you were dead," Johnny said softly, with that bewildered-zombie expression still clouding his face.

I was shivering like crazy. Johnny helped me out of the shower and sat me down on the bed. He dried me off with a towel and removed my wet clothes, pulling my tank top off my skeletal frame and wrestling my soaked jeans to the ground. He rubbed the towel over my shoulders and legs while I shook. He dried my hair gently.

I was getting warmer, but my face still felt wet. I wiped it on the towel, but a second later, it was damp all over again. It took a minute, but I realized what was going on. I was *crying*. Sobbing, in fact. Tears streamed down my cheeks, and I was shaking back and forth inside Johnny's thin arms.

"Oh no. No, no, no."

"Shhh," he said. "Leila, it's okay. You're okay now."

I gasped for air. "Am I?"

I pulled back and looked Johnny in the eye. "Yeah, you are," he said. "But you can't ever do that again, okay? By yourself? This shit is dangerous. I told you that."

I nodded. I apologized, an understatement, for ten thousand reasons. Johnny wiped the salty eye juice from my face. I was naked in his arms—for the first time ever, I realized. Johnny kissed me on the lips. I dug my fingernails into his skin and pulled him toward me. My head pounded, but I didn't want to have to think about anything at all. I meshed my face with his, and our tongues grappled, forcing everything else into the background. Johnny fell toward me, pushing me onto the mattress. He ran his lips down the length of my neck while his hands sought out any soft parts that were still on my body. I pulled at Johnny's shirt, and he expelled it, pressing his chest up against mine. Next came his pants, and then it was sharp hip bones against sharp hip bones, a fencing match in a Murphy-bed arena. I felt his teeth gnaw at my sternum and his hands come up around my throat. I dug my nails into the parchment skin of his back until I drew blood, and I felt him bury a gasp in the bones of my chest.

The sex I finally had with Johnny was rough and ravenous, but I couldn't keep my eyes open and I fell asleep midway through it. When I awoke sometime later in the pitch black of night, Johnny was in the corner of the trailer holding a lighter beneath a metal spoon.

CHAPTER TWENTY

The band was called Say Tin!, and they were Johnny's and my saving grace. Or at least they were the reason we were able to hang around the desert for a bit longer without having to make a sick, sweaty drive back to Los Angeles. Because while moonshine and psychedelics reigned at Camp Kennedy, the boys of Say Tin! were good-and-proper junkies. And they were smart enough to realize that if they were to bring along a little bit of extra dope, they could probably unload it for a premium out in the land of negative civilization.

I met the quartet of black-clad musicians while I was having a cigarette for breakfast and watching the sun go down. They were unloading their gear out of a black Astro van and stumbling around, getting their bearings, behind matching pairs of Ray-Bans. Rex, the not-so-bright high-school friend of Kennedy's, was trying somewhat futilely to manage the situation and make sure the equipment found its way back behind the stage instead of being dumped in the center of the camp, where it might end up covered in any manner of beverage, bodily fluid, or Silly String. The boys were casually ignoring Rex's suggestions, in favor of activities such as yawning, spitting, and taking turns peeing on a cactus.

I smiled at them through the haze of the opiates in my head and offered cigarettes around, a gesture that basically made us blood relatives without having to so much as introduce ourselves. I swiftly sussed out that they needed a place to get high, and invited them to my trailer, leaving Rex to handle moving the equipment with the sheer force of his nervous energy.

If a single nod between me and the boys was enough to solidify a bond, then a mere glance established Johnny as their soul mate. Five minutes after introductions were made, Johnny and the Say Tin! kids were swapping tales of debauchery in Brooklyn, waxing nostalgic about Lower East Side bars, and singing Ramones riffs in a round.

"Oh, 151? On Rivington?" Curtis, the band's charcoal-voiced singer, asked. "Yeah, I've had sex in that bathroom."

Almost in unison, the rest of the boys nodded, implying that they'd had sex in that bathroom as well. I was struck by a twinge of jealousy. Were these guys outdoing me? Were they more dedicated to cultivating the perfect image of waifish depravity than yours truly, the patron saint of tousled hair and razor-sharp rib cages? I didn't have much time to dwell on this possibility, however, because soon enough, cash was exchanged, and Johnny and I had ourselves a mountain of fresh dope—which we swiftly shot straight into our veins.

After an hour spent lying on the bed, running our hands absently across one another's bodies and drifting in and out of being anything at all, Johnny and I walked out to see Say Tin! play for the camp. The band's bizarre logo, a minimalist goat's head, was emblazoned on their kick drum, and a crude pentagram made of twigs was burning on the ground below the stage. I watched them play their dark, dense garage rock with Johnny's thermal shirt wrapped around my ever-shrinking body and his hand clutching my waist. I made eye contact with Kennedy, who stood alone on the other side of the stage, but quickly looked away from his sorcerer's eyes.

With jealousy mingling with opiates in my bloodstream, I made the decision right then and there that the rest of the night would be a motherfucking party. Johnny and the boys missed their precious Lower East Side dive bars? Well, we had an Airstream trailer and twenty miles of earth to destroy. We had beautiful girls and expensive drugs and not a goddamn person in sight to tell us no.

When Say Tin! started playing a dancy Cure-like tune, I looped Johnny's arms around my neck and swayed against him. I lit a cigarette and placed it in his mouth. "Let's go fucking nuts tonight," I said.

Johnny laughed. "Okay," he said in my ear, spinning me around with a display of grace that betrayed his ballet training and made his thin body that much more attractive. I kissed him over and over again, watching that pentagram burn beneath the stage.

After the show, I invited the band to come back to our trailer. I enlisted a few swooning girls to venture forth and track down booze, and told them to spread the news that there was going to be a party at our place.

Johnny and I set up the wine and moonshine on our little table and let the party flow outside. Most of the camp wandered over, with no problem accepting that revelry was the order of the hour. Johnny and I convened once in the bathroom to shoot up, and he winked at me over the sounds of a drunk girl pounding on the door. Then he plunged a needle into my arm, and the pounding faded away until all I could hear was a river of blood rushing through my body.

I was high as fuck and drunker than I'd been in weeks, when Curtis cornered me next to the bush I was using in an ill-fated attempt to maintain my balance. He put his hands against my back and steadied me firmly, like I was a hand truck carrying a load of important boxes rather than simply a human carrying the weight of a million bad decisions. "You want to sit down?" he asked, and I nodded gratefully.

"So," Curtis said once we were seated on the steps of the trailer. "Johnny said y'all are out here doing some kind of research?"

"Yeah, I'm a screenwriter."

"And you're trying to write about *this* place?"

"You don't approve?" I asked.

"Crap like this is so passé," Curtis said. "It's like, yeah, let's go be free spirits in the California desert. Like that hasn't been done a million times. Plus, that Kennedy guy is a real egomaniac."

"How do you know?" I asked, though I knew I wouldn't be able to deny it. "You've been here for, like, five hours."

"Word gets around in the cult world."

"The cult world?"

What do these guys have, some kind of social networking service?

Curtis stood up and peeled off his shirt. The parts of his back that weren't covered in tattoos were marred by cuts, scratches, and burn marks. "I'm kind of a collector," he said.

Before I could respond, Say Tin!'s drummer, an elfish guy named Ryan, joined in the conversation. "I hear Kennedy's planning some sort of ritual-suicide thing," Ryan said. "And he's gonna get a magazine to shoot it."

"No way," Curtis replied. "That asshole loves himself too much for martyrdom."

"So," I said, not wanting to ponder the possibility of a fashion spread full of dead bodies. "Do you guys . . . consider yourselves a cult?"

"We're devoted disciples of the Lord Satan," Curtis said.

I laughed heartily. They were stone-faced. "Wait, really?"

"Nah, that's just for theatrics," Curtis said. "What we're really about is pain. Our MO is indulging in the one thing everyone else is trying to avoid."

"That sounds pretty good to me," I said, surprised to find I meant it.

Curtis and Ryan exchanged a look, excitement catapulting between them. "You want to try it?" Curtis asked.

I bit my lip, wondering what I had gotten myself into.

"Okay," I said, knowing I could follow no other course of action without sending the party on a downward spiral toward the ordinary. "What do you have in mind?"

"Pick a spot," Curtis said. "I recommend the hip."

"Hip it is then."

"Ryan, make fire happen."

Channeling his inner Neanderthal, Ryan gathered a series of twigs and set them aflame. He left for a minute, and when he returned, he was carrying a long metal branding iron and a temporary tattoo bearing that minimalist goat logo. *Oh my fucking God,* I thought, my legs wobbling with anticipatory sickness.

"You sure you want to do this?" Curtis asked.

I nodded, becoming a mute bobblehead of stupidity. I lay down on my side and exposed my hip. I tried to make my mind go blank as Curtis placed the temporary tattoo on my body and spit on it. He pushed his palm against the waxy paper and held it down until the thing had transferred its barnyard evil onto the thin layer of skin that stretched itself over my hip.

Curtis pulled the metal brand out of the flame and held its glowing tip up to his face, which illuminated a demented and aroused grin. He touched the skewer to my skin and began to etch a shape into my flesh. I screamed. I screamed so fucking loud I stopped hearing myself, and my own voice became a signal of pure pain. The louder I yelled, the harder Curtis etched, and I bit down on my hand to keep myself from passing out. It was far and away the worst, most visceral thing I had ever felt, and this was through a filter of opiates. I realized too late that there was nothing at all enjoyable or enlightening about what these guys were doing.

Homemade burn tattoos? Ritual suicide? That was it. I was done with parties, and I was done with cults. That night, as I lay awake choking on the smell of burning flesh that radiated from my oozing hip, I told Johnny I was ready to get the fuck out of the desert and back to LA.

Chapter Twenty-One

INT. CHATEAU MARMONT ROOM - DAY

The curtains are drawn, and the lights are off. Leila
and Johnny lie in bed. Half-eaten plates of room-ser-
vice french fries litter the room.

Leila starts to get out of bed. Johnny pulls her arm.

>   LEILA
>   I gotta get up. I have a meeting.

>   JOHNNY
>   Skip it.

Leila shoots Johnny a look.

>   JOHNNY
>   I mean, really, what's the worst
>   that could happen?

                    LEILA
I don't know. Harlan gets pissed at
me? And has to lie to the studio?

                    JOHNNY
So your Hollywood agent tells a
lie. And? What's the worst that
could happen?

                    LEILA
The studio notices a pattern. And
starts losing faith in me.

                    JOHNNY
Okay, so they get a little worried.
What's the worst that could happen?

                    LEILA
I'm kicked off the project.

Johnny pulls Leila back down into the bed.

                    JOHNNY
Worst that could happen?

                    LEILA
I can't afford to buy us any more
drugs.

When we got back to Los Angeles, I effectively moved with Johnny into a room at the Chateau Marmont. If we pushed aside a few tree branches outside our window, we could see an enormous billboard advertising premium jeans. A man broods in sepia tones, wearing the smallest size of raw denim, a hiss of scruff splashed across his high cheekbones. His slit eyes stare directly into the camera, yet he still manages to set his gaze on something a thousand miles in the distance, perhaps a single Pepsi can floating in the middle of the Pacific Ocean. It was classic Johnny, and I told him daily that he had never looked better.

Johnny immediately booked a guest-starring role on a new series about cybercrime, playing an identity thief who heists everything from a nice middle-class family and ends up crumbling in a hail of gunfire during a shoot-out on a beach near the Mexican border. The day Johnny filmed the beach scene, I bought him a pair of the darkest sunglasses I could find and wished him luck not exploding under the sun.

I was supposed to be starting my first draft of the cult movie, but my heart just wasn't in it. I couldn't really remember what the thing was supposed to be about. Every time I thought of my protagonist, I saw Kennedy's impassive face, unwilling to let me win as I undid the buttons of his pants. I didn't particularly feel like sitting with that image, so instead of working, I shot more drugs and told myself I was letting the themes of the movie bang around inside my head.

I avoided everyone I knew. I would sneak into my apartment only when I knew Mari wouldn't be home, and once I was there, I'd grab the things I needed so hastily it felt like I was stealing them. On one such trip, I saw that her car was still parked out front, so I drove mine around the corner and waited. When her car finally peeled out, I walked up to our door, and as soon as I pushed it open, I heard something move.

"Mari?"

It was probably the mouse, or the mouse's offspring. I did a cursory check to see if the little guy was around. "You in here, vermin?"

Nothing.

"If you're here, I want you to know that you're free to take my bed-room. It's all yours. The bed, the blankets. Anything your little vermin heart desires."

I walked into my room and swiftly gathered some essentials. I couldn't bear to look at my desk, where notebooks full of old writing were piled high. I tried to avoid the gaze of the Virgen de Guadalupe while I threw T-shirts into a bag, and I couldn't help but feel she was trying to avoid eye contact too.

Johnny and I ended up at the Chateau because he'd been gifted a room for a couple of nights by the jeans company whose billboard stood next to the hotel, and once we were there, we didn't really have the physical or mental wherewithal to move out. I knew our drug use had gotten out of hand, but I kept telling myself that Johnny had been doing this for a long time and couldn't possibly be spiraling into oblivion now. Not with so many things on his horizon and our upcoming project so important to both our careers.

Despite the tenuousness of our situation, Johnny and I were sweet to one another, pretty much all the time. We had sufficient money and contacts so that procuring dope wasn't an issue, and we genuinely enjoyed one another's presence enough that as long as we were high, we could hang around for hours listening to music or playing Scrabble or simply lying on the floor and staring at the ceiling like a pair of honey-mooning snow angels. Once a day, we'd order room service, and if the bellhop managed to get it to us before we shot up again, we'd spoon soup into each other's mouths and split a bottle of Perrier. Maybe all this niceness just came down to the fact that if Johnny and I found ourselves fighting, it would mean we were unhappy, and if we were unhappy, it would mean we had a problem.

During this period, stimulants started to feel like that stable old boyfriend you've outgrown but keep telling yourself you'll come back to once the flame blows out on your new love. Because he's good for you, he turns you into your best self, and you've been with him for so long that you can't imagine a future that doesn't have him in it.

You spot him in old family photos, right there in the dilation of your pupils. The size-zero dress he got you hangs in your closet, just a little too big to wear right now. You can't help but remember how supportive he was on countless projects, and you give him credit for how you got to where you are today. He made you prioritize achievement and success. He made you care about being a person worthy of calling yourself a person. So you go back to him for a day every once in a while and hope some of those old feelings are still there.

I felt this need to return to Mr. Amphetamine before a lunch meeting Harlan set up to discuss the status of the cult movie. I took a whore's bath in our room at the Chateau, swiped on some makeup before deciding I'd looked fresher without it, and snorted ninety milligrams of Adderall. The drugs hit me while I was walking to my car, and really kicked in just in time for me to realize I didn't *have* a car—at least not one that was parked anywhere near the Chateau. I made a mental note to have Mari check on my vehicle, which was likely putting in some time as a bird latrine outside our apartment. I had the concierge call me a cab, and spent the ten-minute ride down Fairfax furiously trying to force myself to give a shit about anything.

Harlan was biting his tongue from the moment he laid eyes on me. We sat at a table near the window, and I had to force myself not to squint in the sunlight. When the waiter came by, Harlan placed his order without consulting the menu.

"Just a coffee for me," I said when it was my turn.

"Order a sandwich," Harlan said.

"Do you have grilled cheese?" I asked the waiter.

"We do. A trio of Gruyère, pepper jack, and cheddar that comes on brioche, with a side of house-made potato chips."

"Yeah, that's fine."

I put my paper napkin on my lap to keep myself from systematically tearing it to shreds in full view of Harlan. My fork fell off the table and clanged loudly against the floor.

"So," Harlan said, after watching me try to settle in without knocking anything else over. "Dare I ask how the script's coming?"

"It's good," I said. "I mean, it's in process. I did a shit-ton of research out in the desert, as I'm sure you know."

"How could I not? You were gone for fucking ever."

"I was getting really good stuff."

The expression on Harlan's face read, *I'll bet*, but he didn't say anything at all. The waiter returned with my coffee, and I mixed cream into it quickly, hoping the ground-up beans would be the thing that finally snapped me into alertness. I sipped and swallowed, but my brain remained somewhere else.

"And what's your ETA for it?"

"Huh?"

"Time frame. When will you be done?"

"With the script?"

"Yes." Harlan sighed. "With the script."

I looked into my coffee and tried to appear pensive, like I was mulling over the answer to his question and not figuring out how to avoid it. "Haven't you learned by now not to ask a writer when she'll be done writing?" was what I came up with.

Harlan sighed again. "Can I ask you something personal?" He didn't wait for me to respond. "Are you fucking Johnny Isherwood?"

The shock I felt when Harlan asked the question wasn't over the fact that he knew about me and Johnny; it was because he *didn't know* about me and Johnny. A thrill snuck up my spine as I realized that the life I was living was still somewhat shrouded in mystery, and therefore not nearly as neon as I had feared. Turning this over in my head made me smile reflexively—but Harlan took it the wrong way.

"Oh my God," my agent said, leaning back in his chair. "You're in love with Johnny Isherwood."

• • •

My lunch meeting with Harlan spurred me to double my efforts at avoiding everything in the world. I half told myself it was because I was going to buckle down and get to work on the script, and I one-tenth believed that was going to be true. But my notebooks remained unopened and Final Draft never even saw the light of day. Instead of working, Johnny and I would lie around with blackout curtains pulled over the window and listen to music. I became a scholar of '70s pro-topunk, writing theses in my mind on the Modern Lovers, Television, the Stooges. I spent more time talking to Iggy Pop than I did anyone else save Johnny, who became proficient at singing to me in these per-fect Jonathan Richman and Tom Verlaine impressions. I wouldn't say that Johnny and I were happy, necessarily, but we were content with our small existence made of dope and music. We felt no allegiance to time; what was probably only a week's vacation in Ignoreland felt like months.

Our routine was interrupted when Johnny booked another guest-starring role on a TV drama and forced himself to enter the world like a normal human being, while I stayed behind with the curtains still drawn. Every morning when Johnny left for work, I'd tell myself I was going to go out that day too. The two of us would rise and shine with a cup of coffee and a morning shot of heroin. Then Johnny would give hygiene the old college try, kiss me on the head, and take off to meet the driver the studio provided for him as insurance that he'd actually arrive at the set. Usually I'd make an attempt to clean myself up as well, before ending up back in bed with a well-memorized record lulling me into oblivion. If I did manage to push myself out of our cavernous room, it would only be to take a stroll around the Chateau grounds with a cigarette dangling from my lips.

Thirty-six hours was the longest stretch I went without leaving the room. I had been keeping track, and as soon as I hit that mark I forced myself out of bed. After showering for the first time in days, I put on a cashmere sweater that would have been far too warm for any-one with an ounce of body fat. My hair had been towel-dried, and it was offering its last beads of dewy moisture to the patches of sun that peeked through the dense Chateau foliage. It was a beautiful day, and I actually felt pretty good. I was lighting cigarette number who-knows, my mind eternally somewhere else, when a voice called out from a few feet away. "That's the wrong end."

Almost embarrassed, I flipped the thing around and made it spark. Then I looked over at the voice's owner, a man sitting at a shaded table, reading the newspaper with an enormous cup of coffee in his face. He was handsome, with silver hair and an arm full of tattoos. I recognized Tim Mooney right away and probably would have blushed if there had been any spare blood inside my body. He was one of my favorite writers, and his junkie memoir, *Death of the Day*, had been turned into a Johnny Depp flick more than a decade ago. I remember reading the book as a preteen and feeling like the movie didn't do justice to Tim's vicious and dirty prose. It didn't capture the poetry he'd managed to eke out via descriptions of trying to burn the germs out of dirty toilet water before shooting it into his screaming veins.

"Yeah, I did that on purpose," I said. "Makes it easier to get cancer."

Tim let out a surprisingly hearty laugh. "Makes your cough better too, I bet."

"You should see what happens when I light my own hair on fire. The surgeon general actually flies in to have me personally committed."

Tim lowered his coffee and pushed his newspaper ever-so-slightly aside. "What brings you out and about on this godforsakenly pretty morning?"

"I live here," I said. "How cool is that?"

Tim laughed again. I inhaled my cigarette and smiled. "Hey, do you drink coffee?" he asked. "I could go for a fifth cup."

We walked to the hotel restaurant's outdoor patio and settled into a table. "Four coffees," Tim said to the waiter. "And some pastries and crap."

"Are we expecting company?"

"Nah, I took the liberty of ordering you two cups. They're damn slow around here."

"I like your style, Tim."

"Hmm. I was pretty sure I hadn't gotten around to telling you my name."

"Fuck."

Another chuckle. "Like you said . . ."

"I like your style."

Tim and I continued to make quippy small talk throughout breakfast. I downed both cups of coffee and forced myself to eat half a croissant, for show. I tried my best to keep my eyes alert and undroopy, all while avoiding any line of chat that touched on the personal. Even still, I saw that Tim was noticing things about me without even trying. I knew his ex-junkie eyes saw me in infrared—as if each move I made were passing through an X-ray that betrayed my decaying skeleton— but I stayed there talking to him anyway. Tim had an easiness about him, an attitude that I interpreted as being casually accepting and nonjudgmental.

I was wrong. The next time I saw Tim, we were both guests at a party inside one of the Chateau's bungalows. Johnny had recently met with the potential producer of a new fake-indie looks-shitty-but-requires-a-big-budget project his agent had been trying to get off the ground for months. The producer was a rich geek in his thirties who clawed at the lifestyle Johnny embodied with every fiber of his expensively tailored yet somehow still ill-fitting sport coat. So when he invited my beau to a bash he was throwing right in our very backyard, Johnny decided his best course of action for landing the gig would be to give the guy the pure Hollywood lifestyle for all it was worth— which meant donning his best $200 plain white T-shirt, sliding into his most prebattered leather jacket, and bringing along his very authentic heroin-chic girlfriend.

To prepare, Johnny and I shot speedballs and traipsed around our room to *Some Girls*. I drew thick black liquid lines above my eyelashes and stepped into five-inch heels. I treated the night as if it were a game to be won—and the cocaine rushing through my bloodstream was by no means an unwelcome member of my team, recently shunned as it may have been.

The party was full of Hollywood businessmen and almost-models. As soon as we helped ourselves to flutes of champagne to take the dryness out of our mouths, Johnny tracked down Steven, the producer of note, and introduced me. I held out my hand to be kissed, like the asshole I had decided to play for the night, and Steven was delighted. He slobbered onto my skin and told Johnny I was "lovely"—an adjective I hadn't elicited in quite some time.

The models were dancing to something pulsing I'd never heard before, or maybe had a million times. They all fixed their eyes on Johnny, who leaned so smoothly into the corner of the room it seemed like he was part of the plaster. "Care to swing-dance?" Johnny whispered in my ear. "Maybe a little two-step? I hear you're a natural at the cha-cha-cha."

"Easy, ballet boy," I said. "Before I make you do a pirouette."

Half an hour later, I abandoned Johnny to a boring conversation with someone from his agency and wandered through the rooms of the bungalow. The place was basically a freestanding house, with chic upholstery that probably had to be cleaned as often as a baby's bib, and mirrors on every wall. I downed my champagne and walked upstairs with the intention of giving my ankles a respite from standing at five inches of attention.

I spotted Steven sitting in one of the bedrooms with a smattering of other rich guys. They were crowded around a mound of cocaine and took turns inhaling lines with a hundred-dollar bill. I smiled at Steven, and he beckoned me into the room, introducing me as Johnny's beautiful girlfriend, Kayla.

I grimaced. *Hasn't he heard of me?* I permitted myself to think, remembering that I was supposed to be playing an asshole. I shook a few hands and took a seat at the table when it was offered to me.

The men talked budgets and box offices and passed the rolled-up bill around. "Go ahead," the guy next to me said as he handed me the fucked-up Benjamin.

I looked at the mound of cocaine, all snowy white and wholesome-looking as a fresh Aspen day. I was way past the point where snorting drugs held any appeal for me. It was a waste of time and a waste of money, and, damn it, I had a needle right there in my silver leather handbag. But I couldn't just whip out a medical syringe in the middle of a Hollywood party like it was a business card. I thought about sneaking some coke into my own bill and excusing myself to the bathroom, but there seemed to be no graceful way to do that. I considered sucking it up, and, well, sucking it up, but swiftly nixed the bullshit idea of nasal ingestion. Finally, I did the only thing left on my list of options. I turned to the crowd of stiff, too-loud producers, all bravado and dripping insecurity, and said, "Hey. You guys want to see me shoot this up?"

There was a flash of silence as the group registered what I'd said and considered the sincerity of my offer. I saw curiosity, if not awe, creeping across their faces. "Hell yeah!" one of the guys shouted, and the rest of the men chimed in with their affirmations.

I nodded. I rose calmly and headed toward the bathroom to fill my spoon with water. Out of sight, I mixed in a little heroin. I walked back to the bedroom, where the men were silent and anticipatory. I wrapped my legs around one of the guys, a pudgy and prematurely balding character, and removed the silk tie from around his neck. I secured it across my own bicep, and the man gulped. I dumped a moderate amount of cocaine into my spoon and heated the mixture with a lighter. I could feel all the hungry eyes in the room watching me, contact lenses salivating saline. These guys were ready to live vicariously through whatever reaction I had, and the asshole in me decided to make it worth their while. "Ready?" I asked.

I felt the men draw a collective breath as I stuck the needle in my vein. I pushed the plunger down, conjuring a cloud of blood, and sucked the mixture into the syringe. I released and expelled the drugs into my bloodstream.

Slowly, I inhaled, magnifying the ecstasy I felt for the benefit of the men. I let my eyes flutter and my mouth part. I moaned ever so lightly, oh so delicately. Then my head fell back with a thud, and my body slumped down into the chair.

The men looked at each other cautiously. My body spasmed. More cautious looks came my way, which sent out more spasms. With my head tilted back, I started to slump lower and lower in the chair, until I reached the end of the seat, at which point I fell off with a thud. My body shook on the ground, and my head slammed against the leg of my chair. The men stared with their mouths open.

"Oh *fuck*!" one of the guys finally said. "Is this bitch OD'ing?"

At the mention of the word, the room morphed into a full-on panic zone. No one could take their eyes off me, but no one wanted to touch me either.

"Do we call an ambulance?" one of the men asked.

"Hell no. That shit'll be on TMZ in an hour."

"What about the concierge?"

They considered that one for a moment.

"Let's just fucking go!" It was Steven who spoke. Steven, with his carnal longing for danger and edginess. "And close the goddamn door!"

At that, I stopped shaking and took a deep breath. The guys instantly grew silent, and the asshole I was playing laughed, feeding on the shock that was vibrating from wall to wall.

"Fuck you guys," I said, opening my eyes fully and sitting back up. "You fuckers were just going to leave me for dead."

Pure quiet now. The awe was still there, but it was mixed with something else: horror, I believe. As I stood up to go, repacking my kit as slowly as possible, I saw Tim standing in the doorway with a paper cup of coffee in his hand. There was no awe in his face and no horror either. There was just recognition of the very illest sort.

. . .

The third time I saw Tim, I figured he'd been waiting for me. It was a morning a few days after the party (or afternoon, if you live in a normal-person time zone), and I was out on another of my aimless cigarette strolls. I hadn't showered this time, and I wasn't feeling nearly as high as I would have liked; my skin was crawling. I saw Tim's silver head as soon as I rounded the corner, and I watched him put his newspaper away the moment he spotted me. "Coffee," he asked, although it wasn't really a question.

We sat down at the same patio table as before. This time, Tim ordered us three cups apiece, a sign that it was going to be a while. But instead of talking, instead of laying the spiel I'd been anticipating on me like a chemical weapon, Tim just watched me sitting there across from him. I fidgeted like a virus. I lit a cigarette and let it burn. After five minutes, I couldn't take it anymore, and I exploded at my breakfast companion. "What the fuck?"

Tim shrugged. The waiter brought over a basket of pastries and a cup of orange juice. Tim took a sip of juice and reached into the pocket of his jacket. He dumped a bunch of white capsules out on the table. I didn't recognize them. Then he pulled out a small vial of liquid with a complicated and menacing label.

"Hepatitis C," he said, swallowing one of the capsules with a pull of orange juice. "Do you have it?"

I shook my head.

"You will soon enough."

"I don't share needles," I said defensively.

"Neither did I." Tim laughed hollowly. "Until I did."

"Look, I don't even really have a problem. I mean, yeah, I shoot drugs, but I—"

"Can stop anytime I want?"

"I wasn't going to say that," I said, even though I was. "I'm not that much of a cliché."

"We're all that much of a cliché," Tim said.

"Poetic."

"Exactly my point."

"Okay, fine. You think I'm a junkie, so I must be a junkie. How grand. I appreciate your little silent intervention or whatever, but I know what I've gotten myself into. And when I need to, I'll get myself out of it."

"Look, Leila. You're smart and you're beautiful and you're talented."

I laughed.

"I'd like to think I'd be having this same conversation right now if you were stupid and ugly and inept, but I probably wouldn't be."

"That's a good line. Don't forget it."

"I'm not going to say I care about you, but I do like you. And unfortunately, I know right where you're headed."

"To a life of lighting cigarettes on the wrong end."

"You have a problem."

"Inhaling carcinogenic paper and sucking on wet tobacco."

"You won't let yourself see it, but you have a problem."

"Little girl lost, forever with those backwards cigarettes."

"Maybe no one has told you that yet, but now I have, and I'll tell you again. You. Have. A problem."

"Fuck you," I said and lit a backwards cigarette right in Tim's face.

CHAPTER TWENTY-TWO

Burnt Sienna was always my favorite crayon. While the other little girls in preschool were greedily snapping up the Shocking Pinks and Mountain Meadows, I would render whole landscapes in a monochromatic Burnt Sienna. Dark brown with flecks of rusty red, it's the color of my hair during those periods I spend any amount of time in the sunlight. As a teenager, I briefly considered becoming a Suicide Girl, solely because I was enraged that none of the existing tattooed pinup babes had chosen the glorious crayon as their nickname. *Burnt Sienna, eighteen years old, from Los Angeles, California.* So you'd think I'd have been pleased when I returned to the Chateau after a dope run, opened my fresh bundle of tinfoil, and discovered that it contained a gram of chopped-up crayon in a hue none other than my precious Burnt Sienna. But, against all logic, I was not pleased at all. I was fucking pissed.

My plan had been to wait for Johnny to get home before setting out to score, like I usually did, but his shoot was running late and I figured I'd make like a good little domestic partner and have the dope waiting for him when he returned—all purchased and prepared and laid out, needing only to be heated up. I didn't have any phone numbers, but there was a taco truck downtown where Johnny and I had procured heroin a few times, so I asked the valet to fetch my beau's car from the parking structure and drove over. I circled the block a few times like some kind of private eye before deciding to park a couple of blocks away. I knew I was in over my head immediately, but the pull of the opiates was too hard to resist. With nervousness coursing through my body, I walked to the lot where the truck was parked, as if I were carrying the weight of the act I was about to commit on my shoulders. It was making me shuffle, stooped-over and low to the ground, a cockroach ready to be crushed by anyone who happened to see me.

I strolled up to the taco truck. I didn't recognize any of the three guys inside, but that didn't mean I hadn't seen them before. I hardly recognized myself anymore. I smiled at the man behind the counter, then quickly changed my facial expression once I realized I was trying to sell myself as a heroin addict and had better not reveal that I still had all my teeth. I tried to remember what Johnny had said to the guy to let him know it was dope and not carne asada he desired, but I was drawing a blank. I perused the menu and asked, "What else do you have?"

The man behind the counter shrugged. "You a vegetarian or something?"

"No, that's not what I mean. I was here before, and I got something . . . else."

"You remember what it was?"

"Yeah. But it wasn't, like, *normal*, you know?"

"You like green chile? We can put that on whatever."

"No, I mean like . . . something *else*. Altogether. Not food."

The guy just stared at me like I was standing before him in a straitjacket.

"Um, one second," I said.

I stepped back from the truck and tried to figure out what to do. I could text Johnny and ask for the right thing to say, but that might come off as desperate, and I was trying to make it seem like my decision to avoid waiting a few more hours for him to get off work was actually an act of sweetness and consideration, not straight-up dope-fiending. I looked helplessly around the lot. Out of the corner of my eye, I saw a kid who looked to be about sixteen. He beckoned me over with a thrust of his scraggly goatee. I lit a cigarette and sauntered over like Casual was my family name. I leaned up against the wall near the kid and looked at him out of the corner of my eye. "Chiva?" he asked.

I nodded, and the boy leaned in closer. "Drop your money on the ground and walk to that alley over there."

I took the last two cigarettes from my pack and put them behind my ear. Then I stuffed my bills into the empty cardboard box and casually placed it on the ground for the kid to pick up. He took off, and I finished my cigarette before doing the Casuals proud again by strolling over to the alley the kid had gestured toward. Ten infinite minutes went by before he pedaled over on a little girl's tricycle and placed a bundle into my hand. I stuffed it into my jacket pocket and walked quickly to my car, paranoia lurking in every step. When I was nearly back to the hotel, I allowed myself to relax. I grinned, pleased at my own self-sufficiency.

I paced the hotel room, waiting for my Johnny to return. I figured I owed it to myself to sample my wares before he got back—reward therapy, because I had done such a good job and all. I got out my kit and bleached my needle. I arranged my cotton ball, my spoon, and my lighter in a neat little row on the nightstand. I went to the sink and poured water into a glass. Then I removed the bag of brown tar from my pocket and opened it up.

For a few seconds, everything was fine. I was still getting a dizzy prehigh from anticipation, which simply increased when I unwrapped the tinfoil. It was only when I brought the chunk of dope up to my nose that I began to suspect something had gone wrong. Instead of the sticky-sweet aroma of burned brown sugar (heroin is basically just dessert, after all), this dark mound released a scent that was more chemical, more sterile, than what I expected. At first, I thought it was new-car I was picking up on, but my senses quickly latched on to something else—the smell of something that had, very long ago, actually been inside my nose. No, not speed or cocaine. Long before she even knew what those substances were, young Leila was destroying her nasal passages by shoving them full of crayons, sketching streaks of foreshadowing on the inside of her delicate proboscis. I always was pretty fucking gross.

Still, I was in denial that the smell emanating from my chunk of brown heaven truly was that of crayon. I was enough of a heroin novice that I figured this batch of tar must simply have been cut with something unfamiliar. So I tapped a small chunk onto my spoon and mixed it with water. But when I held my lighter under the spoon, the substance didn't melt with beautiful ease to mingle with the shot of water. It sat there like an angry, useless blob, releasing its waxy scent up into my nostrils tenfold. Fuck.

I looked at the tinfoil package in disbelief. I grabbed one of my notebooks from the spot on the desk where it had remained untouched for weeks and opened it to a blank page. I took a chunk of the supposed tar and dragged it across the paper, where it left a thick trail of rusty brown. "Burnt Sienna," I said out loud and laughed bitterly to no one.

I poured the rest of the crayon chunks onto the bedspread and used them to draw a crude picture on a page of the notebook: a triangular house with a picket fence beneath a giant sun, all of it brown. I gave the sun a pair of Ray-Bans, and then I packed up my kit, hid the tinfoil at the bottom of the trash can, and resumed my act of waiting patiently for Johnny to return so we could go out and score.

And score we did—real drugs—that night, and the next, and the one after that as well. Slowly, winter burned through itself, and the ashes of February blew around in the Santa Ana winds until they resettled as March. This particular month came to us as Los Angeles's version of hell. The last gasps of the year's demonic winds coincided with an unseasonal heat wave, and it made the air seem thick and charged with poisonous molecules. Ants who couldn't take the torture of being underground marched to the surface in droves, attacking every kitchen and outdoor patio in the city. Fortunately for me and Johnny, our tiny hotel room didn't have a kitchen, and I had mostly abandoned even those daily strolls around the hotel's grounds.

By this point, the cult project was in the process of falling apart—at least on my end—as I hadn't turned a single hieroglyph of writing in to anyone. I wasn't returning phone calls, and, although my specific whereabouts were unknown, it was generally assumed that I couldn't be anywhere good. Harlan had arranged one last-ditch attempt to allow me to redeem myself and hang on to the project, an invitation to a Passover dinner at exec producer Jerry Weinbach's Beverly Hills home. I was to charm the shit out of him, summon the sequined Leila Massey that once was, and beg for my supper.

The day of the party announced itself with a clichéd harbinger of doom, a tiny dead sparrow dragged beneath our window by one of the Chateau's resident cats. The creature had been young and dainty, with a small head and a long tail that made me imagine two feathered bridesmaids holding it up as the sparrow stepped slowly down a long aisle. An infantry of ants wasted no time attacking the corpse, and the sparrow was soon completely covered in a coat of shining black. I pulled the curtains closed and paced around the room. "What time are we supposed to be there?" I asked Johnny.

"Before sundown," he said. My least favorite time of day.

I walked over to one of the room's mirrors and took a long look at my face. Pale skin, undereye tote bags, hollowed-out cheeks Calvin Klein would have thrown a black-and-white fit over. I sucked in a huge gulp of air and exhaled it toward the mirror, nearly blowing my reflection away.

"You okay?" Johnny asked.

"I'm kind of nervous," I said.

Johnny paused for a long time before he nodded his head. "Me too."

It was the first time Johnny and I had acknowledged that our current situation might not resemble the perfect picture of health and happiness. But finally saying it out loud—merely hinting at the truth that I was not only petrified of leaving our hotel room and interacting with people but unsure if I was physically capable of doing it—didn't make me feel any better.

"Okay," I said, my doe eyes inadvertently growing as round as they could get. "So what do we do?"

"I don't know."

Johnny hugged me to his chest and ran his fingers through my unwashed hair. Instead of opening up the lines of communication to formulate some kind of escape plan, or at least get the ball rolling in that direction, I chose to see Johnny's display of affection and raise it. I lifted my chin up toward his face and felt my eyes narrow and darken. I spotted fear in Johnny's irises, but I chose to ignore it. I bit Johnny's bottom lip and didn't let go. I knew he wouldn't feel a thing unless I clenched down as hard as I could, so I let myself draw blood. I mashed my hips into his and pushed up against them.

Johnny grabbed hold of my hair and gathered it into a ponytail, which he yanked upward and away from his bleeding lip, pulling my head just above comfort level until I gasped. Still holding on to my hair, Johnny peeled off the T-shirt and boy shorts I'd been wearing and threw them across the room. He dragged me toward the wall by my ponytail leash and shoved me up against its warm plaster. I slid down until I was kneeling on the floor and undid the button of Johnny's pants with my teeth. He pulled off his jeans and tossed them aside, still holding my head by its hair. He grabbed both of my wrists with his other hand. Then he shoved my skull against the wall with his hips, and for a moment, I was able to forget that we were miserable.

We should have showered before the party, but instead we shot up. My arms were track-marked, and my wrists were bright red from Johnny's tight and unrelenting grip. I sprayed my hair with dry shampoo and stepped into a long-sleeved minidress that was sure to inflict heat-wave suffering on whatever parts of my body weren't otherwise occupied by aches and pains and various oozings. Johnny and I dignified ourselves beyond our worth by brushing our teeth, and then we left for Beverly Hills.

Harlan had absolutely no intention of fucking around with pleasantries; the moment Johnny and I walked through the door, he grabbed me in a death hold of an embrace and whispered in my ear, "Do. Not. Fuck this up."

"Good to see you too," I responded, but my heart wasn't in it. Harlan was right, of course. I had let him down, and his bank account too. Instead of giving me this last chance to fix the havoc I had wrought, he should be deleting my name and number from his files and moving on to the next Hollywood girl wonder. So, hit by a wave of gratitude, I decided that I was really going to try. I would get out there and kiss that producer's ass for all it was worth, and then I'd ask for seconds.

"I won't fuck this up," I said, making sure I was looking directly into Harlan's eyes. He nodded, and I recalled that he hadn't yet met Johnny, so I introduced the boys to one another, throwing in florid descriptions of each.

"Harlan Brooks, past-life agent to Shakespeare himself, meet Johnny Isherwood—who is very handsome."

The men shook hands, and I felt the ground beneath my heels become a little firmer. I could do this. I would play this game for a night, and then I'd go home and figure out a strategy for the rest of the series. Suitably convinced that I could pass for human, Harlan escorted me over to Jerry Weinbach, the man of the hour. We walked past the dining room table, which was all set up for Passover—meaning little Haggadahs for everyone, and dishes of horseradish and gefilte fish. Jerry was reclining against an armchair in his living room, talking to a middle-aged woman who had the stink of studio exec all over her. When she saw me and Harlan coming, the woman excused herself to refresh her glass of red wine and check her e-mail on her phone.

"Jerry," Harlan said, putting a hand on the man's shoulder. "This is my prize-jewel client, Miss Leila Massey."

"You have a beautiful home," I said, holding out my hand. He shook it firmly, and I leaned in closer. "Although it is a little Jewy."

A moment of silence followed, wherein I was forced to consider my fate. Had I blown it already? Had I managed to fuck this up? Fortunately, Jerry burst out with a sharp blade of laughter that shattered any ice that was predestined to form between us. He beckoned me into the chair next to him. "Let's chat," he said.

Harlan slipped away, and I sat down beside Jerry, bare legs crossed and angled toward him. "You really do have a gorgeous home," I said. "And I've always been a fan of Jewy."

"Are you a member of the tribe yourself?"

"Half," I said. "My mom's side."

"Ah. And is she as beautiful as you?"

"Much more so, but the Semite in her would never admit it."

Jerry laughed again, and I chuckled along with him. I let my hand touch his kneecap ever so gently and shifted my body the tiniest bit in his direction.

"So, Leila," Jerry said. "I hate to talk business on this of all days, but I am rather curious about that script. It seems you're having a bit of trouble producing it."

I decided I wasn't going to deny this most obvious fact and settled on another angle. "That's true," I said. "I mean, the storyline is so much denser than I think anyone realizes."

"So you have been working on it?"

"Oh, absolutely. The truth is, I got caught up in my research far more than I ever thought I would. I spent most of the fall living out in the desert with an actual cult. Did you know about that?"

"Tell me more." Jerry sounded intrigued.

"Johnny—Johnny Isherwood—came out with me to do character research. It was so intense out there that we felt like we needed to stay for a while. The leader's this guy named Kennedy who is so completely our Marshall Viner fellow that it's crazy. The trouble is figuring out how to capture his modern vibe without losing the authenticity of the real story. I have all the subtext. I just need to figure out how to make it complement the text."

Jerry nodded thoughtfully. If I didn't know better, even I would believe the bullshit I was spewing. "But you do think you can figure it out?" Jerry asked.

"Absolutely," I said. "I just don't want to show anything until I'm sure it's perfect. That could screw the whole damn thing up, you know?"

Jerry nodded like he understood perfectly, certainly no novice when he came to dealing with the quirks of the creative mind. "Okay," he said finally, emitting a note of satisfaction.

"Okay." I smiled.

"Can I get you a drink, my dear? There's a bottle of red from before your grandparents were born."

"That sounds perfect."

As Jerry walked toward the dining room, I realized that I was grinning—and felt pleased to realize those muscles still worked. *I can do this,* I thought. *Jerry will give me a second chance, and I won't screw it up. I'll leave the hotel, and I'll get clean. I'll work harder than I ever have before. The whole movie is right there in my head, after all; it just needs some stuff moved out of the way before it can be seen.*

I was still wrapped in my shawl of happiness when we all gathered at the dining room table. A few token models had been invited to the seder, and they were trying their damnedest to appear the right kind of bored—not the anti-Semitic kind. I nudged Johnny and gestured in their direction. "Flirt with those girls," I said.

Johnny gave me a surprised look, but he obeyed when I told him to sit at their side of the table. I wanted everyone to see the power Johnny could have over people when he tried. I wanted them all to realize they'd be idiots to give up on us. Harlan was watching me, and I could tell he knew exactly what I was doing. He tossed me an approving nod and settled into a chair at my side.

I ate my entire bowl of matzoh ball soup, even enjoying the idea that I was putting a nutrient or two into my body. I listened with enthusiasm as the Four Questions were read. But by the time the seder was over and dinner was being served, I had begun to feel antsy, the first sign that my body was ready for another dose. I fought it, telling myself there was no way I was going to shoot up here at Jerry Weinbach's house. There was no way I was going to fuck this up, not after I had already come so goddamn far.

My leg tapped through the rest of the meal as I served myself the smallest socially acceptable portion of every dish. When the plates had been cleared away and the coffee put up, my skin was covered in a layer of sweat that had managed to outmatch the generous air-conditioning. I still maintained my promise that I wouldn't shoot up in the house, but I knew I'd need something to tide me over until I could get home. It was all in the interest of not fucking this up.

While Mrs. Miriam Weinbach got the desserts ready, Jerry stood and cleared his throat. "Thank you all for joining me in sampling my wife's unleavened cooking—and for not spitting any of it out."

Everyone in the room, save Miriam, laughed. Jerry continued. "The seder's been sedered, and Elijah has come to drink from his glass of wine. But what Passover meal would be complete without a search for the afikomen?"

The table cheered, gearing up to hunt like children for the hidden symbolic piece of matzoh. "High stakes, of course," Jerry reminded us with a wink. "Hollywood style."

As the group dispersed, I glanced into my purse to see what pills I might have stashed away for a rainy day. There were a few Advil and what appeared to be a breath mint from another decade—nothing suitably narcotic for the likes of me. So I excused myself from the table with my best where's-that-afikomen look of sleuthing on my face. My knees were wobbling furiously. I made them move at a controlled pace toward the stairs, but as soon as I had scaled those steps to the second floor, I ran for the master bathroom, praying no one would see me. I rushed inside, closed the door, and locked it behind me. The whole of me shook. It had been too much. I had spent too many hours out there in the land of normal people, and my body was revolting against what I had put it through.

"I'm so sorry," I whispered as I reached for the medicine cabinet, unsure who I was talking to besides myself. Everyone probably. My hand was unsteady, but I managed to get the cabinet door to swing open. Inside, I saw heaven, sweet narcotic heaven in all the colors of the rainbow. And then I saw black.

PART THREE

Well, Fuck

Chapter Twenty-Three

Sweat. Shit. Bleach. Urine. Windex. Disinfectant. Bactine. Mothballs. Latex. Vomit. Soup.

I'd qualify those as full-on stenches, odors, stinks. And then there are the smells that are coming from inside my body itself: the charcoalish burn of fried synapses, the metallic tang of tainted blood, the festering ball of sickly snot that's lodged somewhere inside my respiratory system, doomed to be ignored for other, more pressing bodily alarms.

The bloody gash on my forehead is a joke. It plays court jester to a king who is the violent cramping in my stomach, subjugating itself to a queen who crawls back and forth across my skin. Then there's Princess Nausea, unwilling to be ignored, and Prince Muscle Ache, whose sweet young bride is a ceaseless spasm that runs from neck to ankle. These royal symptoms laugh at the comic posturing of a bleeding head wound that dares seek attention as a worthy piece of the pain pie.

This is the worst I've ever felt. It takes everything I've got to stop myself from kicking over the nurse who comes in to take my vitals, opening up her skin, and crawling inside her body in an attempt to escape my own. I hate my organs, hate my head, hate every pill and

needle I've ever laid eyes on. I hate God and science and all other people, but mostly I hate Myrna.

Myrna occupies the bed next to me. She's droopy and bleached,
and she appears to be middle-aged, which means she's probably about
thirty. Myrna seems to be suffering from the same smorgasbord of pain
platters as me, but unlike the relative stoicism with which I'm digest-
ing my ailments, Myrna is trying to get through it all by praying. She
prays in English, in Spanish, in a rapid-fire hybrid between the two, all
"*Jesucristo*, I'm sorry. Please help me, por favor." Myrna is wailing and
crying and pleading nonstop, and it's driving me fucking crazy.

When the nurse comes back with another adult diaper and a cup
of water, I ask if there's anything that can be done about Myrna. The
nurse pulls the cloth partition between our beds closed, which does
fuck-all to dull the noise and means that I have to watch Myrna's series
of writhing prostrations as if it were Japanese shadow theater. I want to
yell at her to shut up, but I'm afraid of my own voice. I try smashing
my pillow against my ears, but I have to remove it immediately because
it feels like lead. Itchy, woolen lead. I'd like to fall asleep, but I know
that the mere act of closing my eyes would bring down a torrent of
pain and inner violence so intense it would feel like pure evil eating
me alive. I want to command my body to spontaneously combust, but
I don't have the energy for magic, and so I'm forced to lie awake and
listen to Myrna.

"*Jesucristo,*" she moans. "*Lo siento, mi amor.* I am yours. Take me,
take me, take me, and never bring me back."

• • •

Two hours later, I'm still watching the white paint stick to the wall.
Myrna's prayers have become more sporadic, like she's decided to give
Jesus some time off to go rig the outcome of a football game, leave the
imprint of his face on a piece of burned sourdough, and make a rich
person richer. I'm covered in a sticky sweat that chills me and makes

me hotter at the same time. My legs won't stop kicking involuntarily, and my throat feels ravaged as if by angry wolves. It dawns on me that I'm thirsty, and I manage to prop myself high enough up in bed that I can grab the cup of water my friend the ineffectual nurse brought on her last visit.

I take a sip of water, and it soothes me for an instant. I take another sip and buy myself a moment of gratification. Another sip, another flash of relief. And so on, until it occurs to me that I'm going to be out of liquid soon if I don't pace myself. So I start counting down from sixty. *Sip, fifty-nine, fifty-eight, fifty-seven* . . . I reach zero and drink again, let the act of putting something inside my body placate my nerves and soothe the brain waves that are yelling at me to consume, consume, consume. I count down from sixty once more, and again after that. I cheat and take a sip at fifteen. And then I'm out of water. The pain and anxiety inside my body doubles, and all I can think about is finding something else to drink.

I press the button that pages the nurse and wait impatiently for her to arrive. I double-check the contents of my cup to make sure it's empty. I tilt the waxed vessel back and break the surface tension of the last drop of water with my tongue, pulling it into my mouth. And then, impossibly, I check the cup again.

It dawns on me that Myrna must have a cup of water as well. I look over at the shadowy figure on the other side of the curtain and see that it has become shrunken and listless. My first instinct is to offer Myrna money for her *vaso de agua*, but common sense butts in and I realize both that I don't have my belongings with me and that buying eight ounces of water and a Dixie cup from my rehab roommate while both of us are in the midst of murderous withdrawal sickness would be absolutely and undeniably insane. I stare at the curtain, watch nothing happen for a minute, and conclude that my addled roomie must have managed to coax herself into slumber. I take a deep breath and drag my body up off the bed. My knees wobble comically, and the voice in my head sings, *J-E-L-L-O. It's half-alive!*

I slide open the curtain and see that Myrna's eyes are shut tight. I catch a whiff of septic sweat. There, next to her bed, is an untouched cup of water. My heart starts to race as I work my tapioca legs over to the nightstand. I reach for the cup, but just as my shaky fingers wrap around the waxed paper and lift it to my fiending lips, Myrna lets out a moan like she's rendezvoused with the devil inside her nightmare—and has learned he isn't holding any dope. The yelp startles me and makes me spill the contents of the cup down the front of my dressing gown. Fuck. I slide against the wall and collapse, letting the freezing-cold water seep into my skin.

When the nurse finally comes in, I'm still sitting on the floor next to Myrna's bed, dripping water. My arms are wrapped around my knees, and I can barely bring myself to meet the uniformed woman's eyes. Once I decide to get up, I have to brace my arms against the nightstand in order to stay stable. I push against something raised and firm. When I'm standing at last, I see that it's a blue hardcover Bible—it appears Jesus and his symbolism couldn't stay away from our room after all. "Miss Massey?" the nurse asks. "What's going on in here?"

"I . . . just wanted some more water," I say, letting the words hang in the air for a minute.

The nurse helps me back to my bed and puts me in a dry dressing gown. But instead of getting me another cup of water, she hooks me up to an IV, which provides a constant stream of fluids that enter my body at a steady and controlled pace.

CHAPTER TWENTY-FOUR

I spent my first three rehab days in the facility's detox wing—which I've done the honor of naming "Purge-atory," although the sign's still being made. Last night, a nurse took my vitals and determined that my blood pressure has leveled off enough that I'm no longer at risk for spontaneously combusting and splattering ninety-seven pounds of blood, flesh, and stained bone against the sterile treatment-center walls. After spending a third sleepless night in the dormitory of the damned, I'm woken at 6 a.m. by an efficient knock on my door and handed a sheet of paper that marks out my day into hour-long blocks. You could call it an itinerary, an agenda, or even an appointment calendar, but I'm calling it a class schedule for my first day at Community College for Junkies.

6 a.m. – Make Your Bed

I have to read this twice to be sure I'm seeing it correctly. I am, I realize; I definitely am, and I laugh out loud. I feel privy to some sort of inside joke: a middle finger raised up in acknowledgment of the futility of it all. Because the reality of the situation is, my sheets are drenched

in enough poisonous sweat that I half expect a team of biologists to
march in, take some measurements, and declare the entire block a con-
taminated zone. I've been using my pillowcase to wipe my dripping
nose, which runs so neon I've considered holding on to the slimy stuff
and making a sign: "Live Girls?" My blanket, only tolerable when my
sweating runs colder than it runs hot, is wrecked by the holes my filthy
fingernails made in a desperate attempt to escape from the tomb of
misery that has entrapped my body. Festering in this bed is evidence
of every rotten decision I've ever made—flakes of dead skin begetting
drool begetting tears—but still, I'm being asked to fluff it up and tuck
in the corners like I'm Mary Middle America rising on five hundred
threads to make waffles for the kids before heading to her job at the
bank. I laugh as I hold my nose to keep from gagging on my own
stench, chuckle as I flip my pillow over in an attempt to find the less
crusty side, guffaw as I cross "Make Your Bed" off my list with a giant
shaky X.

6:30 a.m. – Morning Meditation

It's now time for morning meditation, a.k.a. Inspirational Quotes 101,
Platitudes in the Modern Era, A History of Giving Up. We're a room-
ful of people whose bodies are meant for sitting on floors, but still,
there's a hum of discomfort as the hundred or so residents of the treatment facility huddle up on the surface of cold morning linoleum. A
thin man with a goatee sits at the front of the room, the leader of our
predawn festivities. He reads a quote from the AA Big Book—something chock-full of the kind of hope we can meditate on—but my
mind tunes out the moment the guy mentions letting God in. Instead,
I focus on the throb inside my head and try to locate its source. I feel
like it's coming from nowhere, which means it's probably coming from
everywhere.

7:30 a.m. – Breakfast

The thought of food turns my stomach into a quarter-operated horsey ride and closes my throat up like an automated guardrail, but I smell coffee, and that makes the cafeteria seem almost bearable. I scoop a little oatmeal into a bowl for show and pour myself a full mug of dark-black brew. I sit down at an empty table and inhale a trail of steam before I take a sip. The coffee tastes rich and hearty, and it warms me from the inside out. It's the first moment of joy I've felt in three days, and I'm grateful for it, as minuscule and fleeting as it may be. A woman my age, give a year or two, settles down across from me, her tray a heaping mound of fruit and eggs. "You mind?" she asks, and I shake my head, even though the sight of fetal-chicken slop causes the horsey ride to lurch forward again. My stomach bucks and brays.

"You look new. I'm Alice," the woman says. I study her. Her bleached hair shows two inches of dirty roots, and there are scabs on her face, but I notice a little bit of light in her eyes and a dab of color in her cheeks that make it clear this is not her first post-Purge-atory breakfast. I raise my index finger in some semblance of a greeting and take another pull from my mug. Alice tucks into her meal, and I keep the coffee close to my face, praying it will suffocate the smell of steaming egg that wafts off her plate.

I keep drinking, hoping to eliminate just a fraction of the ache in my body, maybe an iota of the fog that's been eating through my head for the last four days. I'm looking to suck down another millisecond of joy. Soon, the mug is empty, and I get up for more. I'm surprised to see there's no line.

I sit back down and poke my untouched oatmeal with a spoon. I take a sip from my refreshed cup of coffee and notice Alice smiling at me. *What the fuck are you looking at?* sits at the tip of my tongue, but I don't have the energy to get it out, so instead I mumble, "As if I weren't dehydrated enough."

Alice sticks a forkful of egg in her mouth and chews. She doesn't wait to swallow before she says, "You don't have to worry about that."

"Huh?" I mutter.

"Caffeine is what dehydrates you."

"Yeah. Caffeine."

Alice grins, her teeth flecked with egg bits. "And all the coffee here is decaf. Of course."

Of course. I freeze with the mug pressed to my lips.

All the coffee here is decaf because I'm at a treatment center for drug addicts, and a sip of caffeine—o murderous caffeine, ye holiest of stimulants—might send any one of us on a downward spiral that ends with dead hookers, robbed liquor stores, and a 911 call to a condemned motel just off skid row. "It was those motherfucking arabica beans!" the unfortunate relapsing soul will yell, cursing the Starbucks siren herself.

I slam my mug down and push it off to the side. I'm livid, morally outraged, but I lack the fortitude to express this, so instead I stick the teeniest bit of oatmeal into my mouth while my brain composes an impassioned pamphlet on patient mistreatment and the audacity of decaf coffee that's sure to make me a folk hero of the rehab circuit for years to come.

9:00 a.m. – Group Session

We congregate for group sessions in the main meeting hall, where we're sorted and collated into groups of twelve. My gaggle is herded to a room with thirteen chairs placed in a circle, like this session is the prelude to some sacrificial rite, perhaps a bloody tribute to the death of free will. I'm the newest member, me and a twitchy man with rotten teeth. We're here to replace the two lucky souls who graduated from the treatment center yesterday and are certainly skipping through a field of daisies with puppies at their feet today.

The twitchy man and I watch each other as if we can see things crawling on the surface of one another's skin. Our group is led by a man named David, a diminutive creature with soft eyes, whose black sweater and square-framed glasses would suggest him to be out of his depth, although it's immediately clear that the opposite is true. Against a backdrop of nervous junkies and downtrodden alcoholics, David's relaxed pose and casual smile reign over the room, drawing all the energy in the circle toward him. *So,* I think, *he'll be the one to sacrifice the lamb.*

"Okay, let's start," David says, and all the mouths in the room snap shut. "By giving a warm welcome to the two folks who have joined our group today. Which means: not saying 'Fuck you.'"

I eke out a smile in spite of myself. "Welcome," someone offers dryly.

David manages to set his eyes on both me and the twitchy guy with the black teeth at the same time. He pushes up the sleeve of his sweater, and I see that his arm is covered in tattoos, thick black letters and symbols that betray a history of rage. I can't help but wonder where it all went. "Introduce yourselves, why don't you," David says to us newbies.

The twitchy man and I both deflect, demure, oh-so-politely allowing the other to go first. When the silence gets too heavy, I speak up. "I'm Lei," I say, inventing a nickname, because I can't bear to say my real name out loud.

10:00 a.m. – Smoke Break

At approximately four and a half minutes a cigarette, with time allotted for walking outside, walking inside, and steadying my hands enough that they can operate a lighter, I figure I can smoke five American Spirits in the half hour we're allotted. Five cigarettes a break, four breaks a day, and that's exactly one pack for each twenty-four-hour period. I've got two cartons to my name—twenty packs—and twenty-seven days left here. So I'm going to have to pace myself.

10:30 a.m. – One-on-One Counseling

Since it's my first real day at Narcotics Anonymous Junior College, I've been assigned a one-on-one session with a counselor to discuss my course of treatment. As I look for the office noted on my schedule, I find myself wishing I had a locker so I could shove myself inside its metal walls and avoid having to face the rest of the day. But here at rehab, the only places to hide are beneath the long shadows of junkies, inside the riverbed scars of speed freaks, or tucked under the concave chests of lifelong alcoholics.

I take a deep breath outside the office of my new counselor and loosen my ponytail, hoping to find some relief from the high-score game of pinball being played inside my skull. I'm about to knock on the door when a tall, lightly freckled woman opens it from the other side. Her name is Megan—and oh, is she ever so very much a Megan. She's Megan from head to toe, Megan from the gloss of her hair to the high-heeled boots wrapped around her feet. She's way too Megan to be working at a place like this, and I become so disoriented, so awash in a surprise tidal wave of Meganness, that I momentarily forget where I am. "You can have a seat," Megan says with a Megany timbre in her voice.

As Megan's eyes flit over my file, I glance at her desk. I spot a framed photograph of a cute teenage boy who wears his flannel button-down open over a black T-shirt reading "Mother Love Bone." The kid holds up a pale hand like he's trying to block the camera, but he can't keep the shadow of a crooked smile from peeking out from behind his shoulder-length hair. His cheekbones are just a little too pronounced.

Dead brother, I realize all of a sudden as I look up at Megan and see that same lopsided half-smile hovering absently on her lips. *I'm going to say 1996, maybe three years after the photo was taken, which would have made him close to twenty.*

Megan circles something in my file and jots down a note. *They had always been close. They stayed close until he died, or as close as was possible in a situation like that. She stood by him even after he stole the TV from her apartment for the third time, she bailed him out of jail and made sure he showed up for his arraignment, but she was also the person he talked to in those fleeting moments when he'd felt like everything would turn out okay if he could just get his shit together for real this time.*

Megan closes my file. I look into the crevices of her softly upturned lips and examine her face. I try to figure out how old she would have been when her brother died. The lines around her eyes say "older sister," but the flakes of purple polish on her fingernails say "younger sister." She wears a forest-green turtleneck, but her jeans are skinny and tailored to her casual runner's thighs. Her shiny ginger-colored hair looks to be natural in hue, although it's also been doused in expensive conditioning treatments and cut by the hands of a skilled professional.

Dead twin brother, I decide, as Megan folds her hands softly and says, "Let's begin."

11:30 a.m. – Lunch

I enter the cafeteria at an angle that won't allow me to see the coffee machine even if I want to; that motherfucker is dead to me. As the fumes of generic allfood reach my nostrils, I'm surprised to feel a pang of hunger jab me in the gut. Although my body is still detoxing, there isn't a damn thing inside of it, and I imagine some of the weakness that hangs on me like a cloak will subside if I treat myself to some nutrition. A certain notion creeps up on me, however, the impulse that I should resist eating and let the pangs that nudge at my stomach turn into an angry, ravenous gnaw.

I remember the thrill of starving myself in high school—I never did it out of vanity or insecurity, but for the rush of light-headedness that would come over me if I skipped a couple of meals. Not to mention that the pills worked better if there wasn't anything in my system to buffer them. For me, embracing hunger was just another way to get high.

But I'm not supposed to be doing that anymore, I realize with such obviousness that I feel entirely confused. That's the whole point of being in rehab. A cloud of dark-gray cartoon hopelessness gathers above my head as I mull this over. I can't just get rid of the drugs; I need to exterminate the desire to feel high. Right? Maybe I *should* write off caffeinated coffee, which means I should definitely give up nicotine. After that, I guess I'll x out chocolate; I haven't eaten any for a while, but I recall a certain fondness for Milk Duds. What about carne asada burritos, sushi, my mother's pasta primavera? Even if the thing I want to put into my body is good for me, does looking forward to the way it will make me feel mean that it's a drug?

My head hurts, my body aches, and I can't tell if I'm being petulant, so I get myself a bowl of soup and suck it down. It lasts five minutes in my stomach before I throw it all up.

12:00 p.m. – Free Time

I decide that I'll allow myself two cigarettes at the beginning of free time, and two at the end of the hour—and if I can't stick to this plan, here inside these last-chance walls, then goddamn it, I'm busting out of this building and walking straight into traffic on the 101 Freeway. I open the door to the designated smoking area and hunch over with my back against the wall, so bone-tired that it feels almost spiritual.

There's a guy standing at the other end of the wall watching a Parliament burn. He looks very much like the male version of me: young but beaten, encased in a cracked, dried-out shell that once protected something shiny. We're both courteous enough to avoid acknowledging the other's presence.

There's nothing to do during free time. All the reading material in the building is program literature, and the selection of movies has been whittled down to a bunch of inoffensive crap that couldn't possibly remind us that drugs and alcohol still exist in the outside world. I try sitting in a chair, but even in my exhaustion, I can't handle the way it feels to stay still. So I pace back and forth like a stockbroker at the closing bell until it's time to smoke my last two cigarettes.

1:00 p.m. – Group Video

The hundred or so chairs in the meeting hall would have been squeaky under ordinary circumstances, but beneath the bodies of addicts in various stages of withdrawal, they're downright symphonic. The video that plays for us is a lecture by Father Martin, an old alcoholic priest whose decades of work educating other addicts have made him a legend in the recovery world. This is explained with a whispered spiel offered by the woman next to me, an overweight forty-year-old with the thinnest hair I've ever seen. Her concern that I might not understand the lessons of the video if I don't know the man's backstory is kind of touching, and I'm especially moved when she flips the guy behind us the bird after he tells her to "Shut the motherfuck up, Elaine."

Father Martin is a white-haired wisecracker with a flat, ruddy face that reflects whatever emotion is projected onto it right back at the audience. He reminds me of my grandfather, a kindly blue-collar Irish Catholic who was good with his hands and always had a piece of chocolate and a wink hidden away for me. I try to remember the last time I saw my grandpa, and it dawns on me that I don't even know if he's still alive.

3:00 p.m. – Group Step Discussion

"Step six," the counselor says. "We were entirely ready to have God remove all these defects of character."

At the pace of a step per day, I've joined the treatment center's ongoing NA discussion midway through its cycle—and needless to say, I am not entirely ready to have God remove all my defects of character. The truth is, I'm not even sure how close I am to *wanting* to be ready.

For the first time since I was admitted to the treatment facility, I allow myself to address the elephant lamp in the opium den: *How the fuck did I get here?* How did I go from being a hyperproductive fire spark at the top of my game to a track-marked burnout barely capable of bathing myself, much less convincing another human to pay me good money to churn out teen-friendly adaptations of fairy tales?

I want to blame everything on the shift in my drug habit, the detour from speed to heroin, but I know that would be oversimplifying the problem. Heroin didn't take me by surprise; I invited it in. I was ready for it, was practically begging for it (you know, before I'd reached the point that I was actually, literally begging for it). The honest truth of the situation is much more involved: I was, and am, completely exhausted by the sum total of the life I've led. And I found myself looking desperately for some kind of permanent vacation from being me. Fairy-tale that, motherfucker.

Hey, this is a start, I think, considering what isn't so much an epiphany as an admittance of something I've secretly known for a long time. And then it happens, the biggest surprise yet: all of a sudden, I find myself just the tiniest bit interested in what the people speaking in this room have to say.

4:00 p.m. – Work

We all have jobs to do at the treatment center: cleaning, cooking (if you've been tested for all the hepatitises and are approved for food-touching, of course), manual labor. As odd as it may seem, working actually sounds appealing to me. Comforting, even. The thought that I can spend a little time doing something other than examining every aspect of my battered being, without engaging in total destruction either, blankets me in relief.

When the man in charge of doling out our jobs asks if I'm up for mopping, I nod with something that I daresay almost resembles enthusiasm. I follow him to the kitchen, where he hands me an apron, a giant industrial mop, and a bucket of soapy water. I wrangle my tools out to the cafeteria floor and pull my hair into a bun so functional it's immediately given a 401(k). I do all these things only to find myself staring blankly into my bucket of water, thinking, *Shit. I don't have any idea at all how mopping works.*

The fact that I don't know how to mop is more than just an immediate logistical problem; it hits me as the total realization that I'm not capable of doing anything at all, really. I lack practical skills in the direst way. I've never set up a utility bill. I haven't installed a wireless router or a cabinet. In fact, I gave Mari a stack of my checks so I wouldn't even have to remember to pay rent each month. When I eat, I order out. I have an agent to handle all my business interactions. A flat tire means calling AAA to fix the problem. Even in college, I made enough money that I had no qualms about taking my laundry to a drop-off service—I don't even know how to separate my whites from my colors.

I've been staring at my reflection in sudsy water for several minutes when the man who gave me my job comes up behind me. I think he's going to take it back, and I experience a pang of depression so intense it feels like I've lost a war. "You'll want to start by sweeping up," he says, grabbing a broom from the other side of the room. "The rest, I'm sure you'll figure out."

5:00 p.m. – Dinner

Walking into the dining hall for the third time today, I'm struck by the thought that prerehab, most of the people here hadn't eaten three square meals inside of a single day once in the last decade. I take a seat in the corner of the room and play a game. As the patients file in, I try to guess the favorite meal of each person—that old culinary standby that never let them down even when drugs and alcohol and other human beings did:

- Mr. '70s Mullet: Bugles and Diet Coke; Flamin' Hot Cheetos on special occasions
- Heavy woman with long pink nails and a walking stick: Campbell's tomato soup
- Sir Beach Hair and Holey Converse: Life Savers, just the red ones
- Iron Maiden T-shirt Man: Ferret food
- Myrna, my old roommate: Powdered donuts, when the methadone was working
- Speed-Freak Grandma: Cheez-Its from 1985
- Shivering Girl in pink leggings and an oversized men's sweatshirt, which no doubt means that all the clothes she brought were too revealing for rehab: Semen

6:00 p.m. – Recreational Time

I walk out to the smoking area and see the same guy from this afternoon burning another cancer stick down to its nub. The male replica of me. I light an American Spirit and he sparks another Parliament, taking maybe five drags the whole time he stands there contemplating its incineration. When his cigarette is out and mine long gone, he finally turns to me, acknowledging the existence of another person in his space for the first time. "You want to play cards?" he asks.

I say yes, even though like with many other commonplace things, I don't actually have any idea how to play cards. We walk into the rec room, and the guy grabs a beat-up deck from a basket of innocuous toys and games that are supposed to offer us entertainment. He finds a table and I sit across from him. He shuffles with shaky hands. "I'm Lei, by the way," I say.

"Damon," he offers as if it were a gift. "Whaddayou wanna play?"

"Um . . ."

"Poker? Blackjack?"

"I don't actually know how to play either of those."

Damon nearly snarls. "Well, what do you know how to play?"

"War." I say.

"War?" Damon rolls his eyes and starts dealing the cards into two piles. "Okay, War it is."

I watch my companion hand out the cards. He wears several rings on his fingers and has a tattoo across his knuckles, the substance of which I can't make out. It's a name, maybe. He's got dark eyes and long, beautiful lashes. His skin was once porcelain but is now marred by acne scars and tiny cuts and bruises. He's wrapped in a faded Levi's jacket, which hangs on him more like a layer of dirty skin than an article of clothing.

Damon throws down his first card. It's an eight, and mine is a ten. I collect. His next card is a seven and mine's a jack. I win his queen with a king. "I'm pretty good at War," I say.

"It's arbitrary," Damon replies. I take two more of his cards. The next round, we both throw out aces, and then we lay down three cards apiece. Damon beats my six with a nine. He laughs sharply.

"Figures," he says.

"What?" I ask.

"Nine."

"That meaningful or something?"

"It's the number of times I've been to rehab."

10:00 p.m. – Lights-Out

By the time lights-out rolls around, I've been in my room for an hour doing nothing at all. I'm exhausted, but I know there's little chance of the strawberry-breathed, naturally blond angel of sleep visiting me anytime soon. My brain conjures up stock images of the rainbow assortment of pills I'd like to ingest to knock myself out. There's red Ambien, orange Xanax, yellow Klonopin, green OxyContin, blue Valium, indigo Lunesta. Shit, even a Benadryl would be welcome at this juncture. But asleep or awake, I'm doomed to make my way sober through another night of torment. I look at my bed, neatly made up and so admirably hiding the horror show that lies beneath its covers. I don't want to ruin my life's sole element of order, so I climb on top of the blanket and settle in for tonight's showing of my new favorite program, *Shadows on the Wall.*

INT. REHAB EXAM ROOM - DAY

Leila sits across from NURSE CARRIE, looking a bit anx-
ious. Carrie flips through a page of lab results.

                    LEILA
          Shit, there is a lot of weight to
          this room. I mean, you're basically
          Saint Peter, but your pearly gates
          are test results.

Carrie looks up at Leila a little sharply.

                    LEILA
          Sorry, I make jokes when I'm ner-
          vous. Bad habit. One of many,
          obviously.

Carrie just nods.

                    LEILA
          And goddamn, am I nervous.

                 NURSE CARRIE
          Well, you should be.

Leila takes a deep breath. Closes her eyes.

                 NURSE CARRIE
          But you're also lucky.

Leila opens her eyes.

                    NURSE CARRIE
        Everything here looks okay. You're
        extremely dehydrated, and your BMI
        is much too low. But your test
        results are all negative.

                        LEILA
        Oh my God. Thank you. I was really
        scared there.

                    NURSE CARRIE
        You have a second chance. Remember
        that, okay? Not everyone gets one.

Leila nods.

                    NURSE CARRIE
        Now, we're going to get some liq-
        uids into you. And I can give you
        some Advil for the headaches, but
        I'm afraid that's all you're going
        to get.

CHAPTER TWENTY-FIVE

Ten long and regimented rehab days go by before I have my first visitor, a fact that doesn't especially surprise me. I can't blame Johnny for not coming, as I'm sure he's still pumping his veins full of ambrosial poison night and day. And I assume the only other person who knows I'm here is Harlan. So it's my agent I expect to see when I enter the common room—appearing out of place while brushing an invisible piece of lint from his suit jacket, or maybe even buried in a phone call. Instead, I see my father. He's alone, and he looks older and more prematurely stooped than I remember. I try to figure out how many months have passed since we've been together, but the task is pointless.

Oddly enough, the first thing my dad comments on is how young I look. And it's true. My hair's pulled back into a clean ponytail, and I'm not wearing makeup. My leggings read as neutral, and I'm a bit dwarfed by the gray sweatshirt I've cocooned around my body. And I've been sleeping, really sleeping, so there's even a bit of color in my cheeks. I appear fresh-faced and innocent, as though my past has been miraculously expunged from my record.

My dad and I stand across from each other, both shuffling around a little until he finally wraps his arms around me and kisses the top of my head. We find an empty table near the window and sit. Neither of us knows what to say at first, and we do a lot of fidgeting. Across the room, a woman with a melting Mohawk abruptly stands and vomits into a potted plant. It's quite the icebreaker.

"Welcome to rehab," I say.

"I'm guessing this is not a place where you ask your neighbors for a cup of sugar much." He pauses. "That's probably drug slang, isn't it?"

I laugh. "There are some great people here, actually."

He looks around the room. "Interesting characters?"

"Definitely. But also just people."

My father nods. I look into his eyes, and he offers me the kindest smile I've seen in a long time. It's so gentle I can see it creep incrementally outward from the center of his mouth. I want to return the favor, but it suddenly feels improper and confusing, like sweetness is no longer something I get to pretend I contain.

"Hey, Dad?" I ask. "How did you even know I was here?"

"A man—Harlan—I guess that's your agent? He came by the house."

The news surprises me. I'm not sure if I feel gratitude or betrayal, or anything other than fatigue, really. It's a strange intersection. I'd always thought I could keep those two groups of people separate, seamlessly compartmentalizing my life.

"Were you and Mom, like, shocked when you heard? I mean, did you know I had a problem?"

"Leila, if we knew you had a problem, we would have done something."

I nod. I believe him. I did have it all together for a pretty long time. And I hadn't been living at home for years.

"Your mom . . . she just couldn't, you know?"

I nod. "It's okay."

"Look," my dad says. "I'm really struggling with how much guilt I should feel. Or responsibility."

"You mean, like, genetically?"

He seems baffled. "I mean, as your parent. As the person who's supposed to be looking out for you."

"There's something I need to tell you," I say. My dad shoots me a look like he isn't sure if I'm going to tell him I'm pregnant with Hep C's baby or secretly working a sting operation as a vice cop. I guess anything's fair game now.

"I read your book," I say. "Your memoir."

My father looks relieved, and then he looks confused. "Wait, my what?"

"Your book. I found it in the garage."

"I'm not sure I . . ." My father thinks for a moment. "You mean my *novel?*"

"Sure. Your novel, your fictionalized memoir, whatever."

"The manuscript about the crazy guy? The thing I wrote when I was twenty-three?"

Hey, that's my age, I think. I'm tempted to grab my father's hand across the table, but I don't. "I really loved it, Dad."

He takes a deep breath and looks me over. "How long ago was this?"

"I was eleven, maybe. Or twelve."

"Jesus Christ."

My father gets up and starts to pace the room. He places his hand against a tree trunk to steady himself, and I cringe. There's vomit in that pot, though my dad doesn't seem to notice. He comes back to the table, but he's looking at me differently now. My gaze must have hardened; the blood must have run away from my cheeks. My past must have reared her ugly head.

"Leila, that book was fiction."

"Well, yeah. All memoirs are, somewhat."

"But it's *not* a memoir. Not by any stretch. It was a novel written by a curious kid. You understand what I'm saying, right?"

At first, I think my dad's trying to pull one over on me, that he's still too embarrassed to talk about his drug-laden past. But I consider for a moment, and it dawns on me that he's probably telling the truth. I study his face and take in the parts where we overlap—the eyes, the cheekbones—but then I dwell on the nose and the lips, capable of such a kind smile, where we veer dramatically apart. Now that I know so intimately what it is to be an addict, I understand there's no way that word could possibly describe my father.

"But you don't drink," I say. "You never drank. Isn't that because you had a problem?"

"I don't drink because I can't stand the taste of alcohol. Never could. It just doesn't do it for me."

I don't say anything. I nod, or at least I think I do. I've gone a bit numb.

"I'm a big old square, kiddo, have been my entire life. That book was just a young man's flight of fancy. A way to do a little experimenting without any real consequences."

"But everything you wrote felt so totally honest. I mean, I've *been* there now."

He winces at the words. It makes me regret them.

"Well," he says, looking down at the scratches that cover the table. "Did you ever think that maybe I'm just a good writer?"

CHAPTER TWENTY-SIX

When I was ten, my class went on a field trip to the Natural History Museum, and I remember spending the day staring transfixed into the gaunt faces of dinosaurs that have existed for the last hundred million years as nothing but a collection of bones. In the ninth grade, my chemistry class took a field trip to Griffith Observatory, and I learned that I would weigh 37.323 pounds on Mars. At the age of twenty-three, after two weeks in rehab, I began taking field trips to an AA meeting inside the squeaky gymnasium of a Hollywood community center.

For us patients, these nighttime journeys are the highlight of our time in treatment and the only occasion when we're permitted to get out from behind the facility's white walls. All rehab upperclassmen who have completed at least half of their monthlong stay are rounded up and buckled into one of the treatment center's three anemically white passenger vans. A hum of taut excitement rides shotgun on these trips, and I can't help but wonder if the point is for us to develop positive Pavlovian responses to the concept of AA meetings—like we're being conditioned to look forward to future treatment simply because it's more interesting than mopping the floor.

I've been surprisingly distracted by the revelation that my father didn't hand any addict genes down to me, though I haven't talked about this to anyone yet. I've fostered something of a tight-knit friendship with my spiritual doppelgänger, Damon—by which I mean I'm currently up twenty-six games of War to his fourteen—but the guy isn't much for conversation. I have managed to glean a few things about his past through careful sessions of coaxing. He comes from a wealthy town in Northern California, entered his first treatment center at the age of eighteen, and once had a Boston terrier named Iggy. His girlfriend Alex overdosed and died five years ago. Damon found her stiff and blue on the futon that served as the sole piece of furniture in their studio apartment, halfway through a *Rolling Stone* article about Courtney Love. The other thing I've learned about Damon is that his family will no longer take his calls on Christmas.

Tonight marks my fifth time attending an off-campus meeting. Our clan is gathered inside a church on Coldwater Canyon, along with fifteen unaffiliated addicts. The session delves into the idea of learning to live with yourself as a sober person. I've never spoken at one of these meetings, and in the time I've known him, neither has my card-game compatriot. But now he raises his hand and stands. "I'm Damon," he says, imbuing his name with the same derisive inflection as when he first shared it with me. "Addict and alcoholic."

"Hi, Damon," we all say. It isn't as funny as it sounds in the movies.

"At this point in my life, everyone I know assumes I'm stupid," Damon says. "They can't understand why I keep ending up like this. Why I won't just stop using once and for all, and learn to behave like a normal adult. But I'm not stupid. I recognize that this is probably my last chance. There are only so many times a person can tempt fate and walk away unscathed, and the odds are no longer in my favor.

"The last time I got clean, I went to stay with my older sister, Leslie. She works in real estate, but she wasn't always, you know, *like that*."

A wave of laughter ripples through the room.

"I'm a musician," Damon continues. "And Leslie's actually the reason I got into it. Christ, it sounds so stupid—but I remember being a little kid and sitting outside her door when she had friends over. That play *Rent* had come out a couple of years earlier, and my sister and her pals were all obsessed with it. They'd put on the soundtrack and sing along to the whole thing, and I'd listen from the hallway, memorizing all these words I didn't even understand.

"In retrospect, it was a funny situation: all these rich white eleven-year-old girls obsessing over HIV-positive junkies and trannies and, like, longing to be *starving artists*. Meanwhile, there's sushi rice stuck in their braces. But for me, it wasn't even about that shit. I just thought it was cool that people could have music playing their whole lives.

"I tried to tell my sister about this when I was staying with her, you know? But she just looked at me like I was still a little kid and not a real person like she was. Like I was stupid. But I'm not stupid, and I don't want to die. I know that I don't want to die. But the thing I can't get over is that without drugs, there are too many silences. There are too many moments that are just empty, that are filler. Living with myself sober is like living without a soundtrack, and I've never understood how people can do that."

• • •

The next day during rec time, I make a beeline for Damon and toss a deck of cards on the table. I'm determined to find out more of the basic things that comprise my friend's personality, and I fire questions at him as we play our daily game of War. "What's your favorite band?" I ask.

Damon rolls his eyes at me, but I can tell he wants to answer. "The Velvet Underground," he concedes. "Bowie's a close second."

I throw down a ten.

"Um," he says. "What about you?"

"The Rolling Stones. Tom Waits."

I win several of Damon's cards in a row. "Favorite author?" I ask.

"Hunter Thompson, I guess. You?"

"Faulkner. James Baldwin. Hubert Selby. And I like Denis Johnson a lot."

Damon wins our first four-card showdown.

"Favorite movie?" I ask.

"My Own Private Idaho."

"Pulp Fiction," I say, and Damon scoffs. "Favorite actor?"

"Robert Downey Junior, probably," he says. "You?"

"Johnny Isherwood," I say with a smirk and throw down a two. Damon wins it easily. His stack of cards has grown so it's about equal to mine.

"Favorite drug memoir?" I ask.

"Permanent Midnight," Damon says, and I have to agree.

CHAPTER TWENTY-SEVEN

Harlan finally shows up at the treatment center, just a few days before I'm scheduled to check out. I have mixed feelings about getting back into the real world, and I find myself uncharacteristically nervous as I walk across the common room to meet him. He's annoyed because the man at the front desk made him throw away his coffee, and it was a bold fair-trade Ghanaian blend.

"Caffeine's a stimulant," I say. "Thus, a drug."

"But not really," he replies. "I mean, come on."

"I know. It weirded me out too."

"It's kind of a priceless rule. You should write it down so you don't forget."

I brush off the comment, even though it bugs me, and wait for Harlan to ask me how I'm doing. He just taps his fingers against his knee. The potted tree has been removed, but the room still smells faintly of vomit from the previous incident. Or maybe that's how this room has always smelled.

"So, how are you doing?" I ask him instead.

"Oh, I'm losing my mind," he says. "This town's a mess. I've got three projects out there about the same thing. Adaptations of gay athlete biographies, but there's no sex in any of them—just a lot of angst and working out."

I nod and offer a little laugh. I glance at the clock and see that it's almost time for afternoon chores. "Sounds lame."

"I tell you, everything's so fucking sanitized right now."

"People tend to puke in this room a lot, so 409 gets dumped in buckets."

"I meant in the industry."

"I know."

"Of course you do," Harlan says. He leans forward and tries to seem casual. "So, how's the script coming?"

"The desert movie? That's still happening?"

"Oh no, they've got a kid from Austin on that now—some film-school cowboy. I meant *your* script. The big one. About your life."

"I haven't exactly been doing a whole lot of writing in here, Harlan. And truthfully, I think I'm ready to put that thing behind me. Cut my losses, etcetera."

"Well, too bad. Because we sold it. Remember?"

I twist my face into a question mark. "We *what?*"

"We sold your damn script. I made the deal at Jerry's seder. You signed on the drive away."

"On the drive *here?* To rehab? I'm pretty sure I was unconscious."

"Nah, you came in and out."

"Harlan." I put a hand to my temple and try to tease away an oncoming headache. "What the fuck?"

"This is good news. Fucking great news. You're supposed to be happy."

I look around the room. A man with neck tattoos plays solitaire, and a malnourished girl compulsively bites her fingernails until they bleed. "Yep," I say. "I'm feeling nothing if not incredibly happy. Ready to plaster my inner joy on the silver screen."

"Oh, come on. Don't get all moralizing on me, not now. This is a thing you wanted, and I got it for you. Okay?"

My headache's arrived, and there's nothing I can do about it. I sigh in a way that's almost onomatopoeia. "I need a break."

"Well, yeah, of course. You can have that. Look, we all understand if it takes a little time. Obviously. But eventually, you'll get up and deliver."

"I mean, I need a real break. From myself. From thinking about this shit, day and night. Plus, the narrative has changed. I found out some stuff about my family that makes the whole first act untrue. Warps the character motivation. And it kind of unravels the whole thing."

"So what? No one said it has to be *true*."

I breathe in. I hear cards shuffling and skin being torn from flesh.

"Leila." Harlan takes my hand and taps it twice. "Do you remember what you said to me the night we met?"

I close my eyes and let the headache drag me under.

INT. TREATMENT-CENTER COMMON ROOM — DAY

Leila glances at the clock. She rubs her temples.
HARLAN leans forward.

                    HARLAN
          Do you remember all that shit you
          told me the night we met?

FLASHBACK:

INT. BAR BATHROOM

Fluorescent lights flicker from above. Lines of cocaine
are spread out on the counter. Leila and Harlan laugh
as they take turns snorting up the drugs.

Leila is clearly wasted.

                    LEILA
          I totally have a plan, you know.
          Yep, I do. And it's a good one.

                    HARLAN
          You keep bringing up this so-called
          plan of yours.

                    LEILA
          Do I? Shit.

                    HARLAN
          Well, you going to tell me or what?

Leila smiles coyly. She leans over and inhales a line
of coke. She swoons a little, her eyes going a bit
wild. She does not look great.

Leila leans forward and steadies herself on Harlan's
shoulder. She places her mouth to his ear.

                    LEILA
                (whispering)
        I'm talking about rock fucking
        bottom.

She sways.

                    LEILA
        Hard-core addiction. Coming to in
        an alley on the precipice of death,
        sleeping it off, then doing it all
        over again. Near misses, 3 a.m.
        revelations. That's the shit people
        want to see.

Harlan looks her over. He isn't quite sure what to
think.

                    LEILA
        And I'm going to give it to them.
        I'm gonna flame out by twenty-five.
        I'm on my way, as it is. I'm gonna
        try every single thing and feel
        every single feeling--my scars are
        gonna have scars, motherfucker!

A devilish grin spreads across her face.

                          LEILA
          And then you and I? We're gonna
          make a movie about it. And this
          town will lose its fucking mind.

Harlan takes a step back. He looks Leila over as she
tries to steady herself against the wall. He grins.

                         HARLAN
          Bravo, you little monster. Just as
          long as you don't up and die on me
          first.

Chapter Twenty-Eight

The ironing board is too long to fit between the door and the armoire that sits in the corner of the light-blue room, so it sticks out a few inches into the doorway—which means I've rammed my hip against its metal point at least a dozen times. I wish I could remember that the damn thing is there, and I also wish I didn't bruise so easily, as my hip is starting to resemble a Rorschach inkblot. But more than anything, I wish that my mother hadn't turned my childhood bedroom into a laundry center.

I've been back inside the house I grew up in for five days, but I still get confused about where I am every morning. Mornings are the hardest. My body has slowly begun to adapt to life without drugs, so falling asleep is no longer a problem for me—in fact, putting my head to my pillow is all I ever feel like doing. The downside of this newfound ability to catch restful, sober Z's is that I have vivid dreams each night and wake up horrified each morning. For years, I had no trouble suppressing every shitty feeling and guilty emotion that dared intrude on my blissful productivity. The result is that my subconscious has become a stratified novelty skull, comprised only of bad thoughts. On the bottom, there's a layer of remorse over having been an aloof and distant daughter from the time I was old enough to spell those words in return for bright-red A-pluses. The next tier starts when my drug use did: there's money pilfered from my mother's purse, countless medicine cabinets raided, lies told to people who did nothing but nice things for me. There's the brazen arrogance I assumed as a cloak of defense, acquaintances I never let turn into friends because I'd felt they weren't good enough for me—weren't as clever, or as fun, or as high. For the first time, I'm acknowledging that I've treated people as tools to be used and discarded once I'd ground them down so much that their points weren't suitably sharp anymore. Or after I'd spotted someone shinier. The topmost, and therefore freshest, layer of my subconscious is an apology to myself. It's made up of the guilt I feel over having taken a bounty of potential and squandered it—or more directly, at having utterly fucked myself over.

The other problem I've developed is that I'm now utterly and fundamentally incapable of envisioning my future. How could this possibly play out? Do I stay clean and move on to another career, maybe go back to school for my teaching certificate and marry a nice lawyer? Do I relapse and lose all my friends—and what's left of my money, my health, my teeth—before I eventually OD? Or am I doomed to play out the last few years over and over again, constantly cycling through recovery and relapse and recovery and relapse and redemption until one time, it finally sticks—for a while, at least.

If I stay clean, will I walk through the world like a shadow of the person I once was, never feeling wholly human? If I start using again, will the success I once had return for a while, or will the lowest depths of my addiction be waiting there to greet me as soon as I pick up a pill or a needle? When I close my eyes, my mind writes blank pages until I fall asleep.

I still have quite a bit of explaining to do. My parents have been walking on eggshells around me, biting their tongues, as though uttering one wrong word could send me right back down the tar-paved road to hell I'd barely managed to veer away from. My dad and I haven't talked about his book since the day I found out it wasn't real, but it's the unsaid part of every conversation. I know we'll have to discuss everything to death eventually, but for now I'm just going to try and get through today.

INT. DINER — DAY

Leila and Harlan sit at a table. Leila sips from a mug
of coffee. Harlan speaks excitedly, his hands flailing.

                    HARLAN
        Off the fucking hook, I tell you.
        I'm fielding ten calls an hour about
        you.

                    LEILA
        How'd that happen? I mean, no one's
        even seen the script.

                    HARLAN
        Hey, word gets out. This idea is
        golden. And you knew it all along,
        kiddo.

Leila signals to the waitress for more coffee.

                    HARLAN
        I'm going to need the pages you've
        written so I can send them to Max
        and Sophia over at the studio,
        okay?

                    LEILA
        Harlan--

                    HARLAN
        They want to start talking about
        getting talent attached. What about
        Michael Pitt for the love interest?

Or that skinny white kid with the
cheekbones from The Wire?

                LEILA
     I mean, shouldn't Johnny play
     Johnny?

Harlan looks away.

                HARLAN
     Johnny's pretty tied up with the
     cult movie, so--

                LEILA
     Oh. He's still doing that?

Leila looks down. Gets lost inside her coffee cup.

                HARLAN
     Forget Johnny. He's a loser. This
     is about you. And kiddo? You are
     about to be fucking huge.

                LEILA
     I just don't know if this proj-
     ect is the healthiest thing for me
     right now.

                HARLAN
     There's a payment sitting in a bank
     account for you right now, and it's
     a fuck-ton of money. I get that
     this is emotional--I do. But you're

not just going to walk away from
this kind of cash.

                    LEILA

But I could. Is the thing.

                    HARLAN

Oh yeah? And what are you going to
do for a living? Practice law? Wait
tables? Kiddo. You don't know anything else. This was your plan. Now
see it through.

Chapter Twenty-Nine

I can smell pancakes cooking, and it makes the thought of getting out of bed and facing the world more bearable. I've gained eight pounds since the day I checked into rehab, and I can see the weight hanging on my body every time I pass a mirror—hunks of flesh I want to tear out and stomp on until they explode into loathsome globs of ooze. But I understand the weight is healthy and that it's my brain that's sick, so I try to keep my focus on other things.

My mouth waters involuntarily at the buttery scent from downstairs. I throw on a pair of jeans and make my bed, something I've continued to do each morning even though I'm out from behind the treatment center's rules and daily agenda. I halfway wonder if I might not take up professional mopping too. *Leila Massey: janitorial wunderkind.* Weirdly uncomfortable with the informality of going barefoot in my own parents' home, I slip into a pair of socks. Downstairs, my mother is flipping pancakes on a griddle. A stack steams atop a blue ceramic dish, new since the last time I ate here.

"Good morning," my mother says, shoving her voice full of extra cheer.

"Hi, Mom." I pour myself a cup of coffee and add a drop of whole milk from the refrigerator.

"Would you get the syrup out?" my mother asks.

I put the sticky bottle of maple syrup on top of a napkin and set the table with a pair of plates and forks. My mother brings the pancakes over, and we both sit in the same seats we would have been found in on any morning ten years ago. Habit is a hard thing to break. "How many would you like?" my mother asks.

"Um, two for now." The pancakes are filled with apples and chocolate chips. It's a meal I ate on five hundred mornings growing up, and the smell evokes cartoon TV and spilled milk and the dread of an impending boring hour spent flailing around on a soccer field with a gaggle of unathletic girls who were just there for the pink uniforms. My mom slides two pancakes onto my plate. "Thank you," I say.

I cut myself a piece of pancake, making sure to get both a chunk of apple and a chunk of chocolate chip. My mother sees me do it, and a smile spreads across her face. I grin sheepishly. "I can't believe you still eat like that," my mother says.

"You have to, Mom," I say back. "Otherwise, it's a total waste. What's the point of putting both apples and chocolate chips in the pancake if you aren't going to get both tastes at once? It's physics."

"Honey, that's not what physics is."

"It's not? Well, I'm pretty sure I got a five on that AP test."

My mom shakes her head, continuing to smile until her lips appear frozen in the shape of a canoe. A silence overtakes us, and I cut another bite so I can fill the emptiness with chewing. I suck down some coffee, all too glad I've been able to introduce caffeine back into my diet, but painfully cognizant of the amount I'm consuming. One day at a time suddenly seems overwhelming, so I change my mantra: *One goddamn bite at a time.*

I flip a third pancake onto my plate, and I can tell this makes my mother happy. I try not to think about the sharpness that has been fading from my cheekbones, and the fact that my jeans feel a little tight around the stomach. I let the syrup swirl liberally on top of the dough and watch it fill the crevices and puddle around the chocolate chips. I make an exaggerated show of cutting up the pancake for my mother's amusement. When I eat, bits of flour make their way into the hole in my mouth that once contained a healthy tooth.

"Hey, Mom," I say, suddenly aware of the stillness of the house. "What day is it?"

"Oh, it's Thursday," my mother says, and then she's busy scraping a mound of chocolate from her plate.

Thursday means that, once again, my mother is staying home from work to look after me, even though she promised she wouldn't do that anymore. "Mom—"

"I was thinking we could go shopping this afternoon. Maybe check out some boutiques on the east side, then head to the bookstore?"

"Oh. Um, I have a meeting to go to. You know?"

My mom's expression falls. "Right."

"But I'll be home later," I say. "We can watch a movie. And hey—what if I help you make dinner?"

"Only if you feel up to it," she says, looking at my face like whatever she sees there still isn't quite what she expects.

INT. BEVERLY HILLS OFFICE — DAY

Leila sits across from two slick executives, MAX (35)
and SOPHIA (40). She seems a little nervous as she sips
from a bottle of water. Max leans forward.

>   MAX
>   So obviously, we don't normally
>   give notes on scripts that aren't
>   finished, but this is a unique situ-
>   ation. And I have to say, we fuck-
>   ing love what you've done with the
>   first two acts.

>   SOPHIA
>   So edgy and provocative.

>   LEILA
>   Thanks, I was aiming for that.

>   MAX
>   So where's it going? How does it
>   end?

>   LEILA
>   You know, I think it's going to be
>   a little vague. Open to the audi-
>   ence's interpretation. Let's let
>   them decide if she gets her shit
>   together or not.

>   MAX
>   Hmm.

                    SOPHIA
Yeah, I don't know if that's the
right move here.

                     MAX
I mean, we want redemption. We need
that for this character.

                    SOPHIA
Do we, though? Isn't redemption
a little played out? Honestly, I
think it makes a better story if
she dies.

                     MAX
Ooooh, I like it. I love it. Leila?
Thoughts?

                    LEILA
I don't know. I mean, of course
I've considered that as a possibil-
ity, but it's so dark.

                    SOPHIA
Exactly.

                     MAX
Dark is making a comeback this
year.

                    LEILA
But maybe a little manipulative?

                         SOPHIA
          Well, it's certainly more dramatic.
          And more honest too, wouldn't you
          say?

                          MAX
          Totally. My God, this could be like
          Romeo and Juliet. Tragic, sexy. A
          classic for the ages.

Leila fiddles with the wrapper on her water bottle. She
shrugs.

                          MAX
          Hey, just think about it. Okay?

                         SOPHIA
          You know, I bet it would help get
          the movie made. Which is what we
          all want, isn't it?

CHAPTER THIRTY

I drive to my NA meeting an hour before it starts and park down the street. Then I walk. That's mostly what I do during the day now: walk, to nowhere in particular and with no real sense of where I'm going. I don't feel like listening to any of the music I used to love before I went to rehab, and my iPod is now mostly filled with blues: Lightnin' Hopkins, Mississippi John Hurt, Robert Johnson, and Chicago-based guys like Muddy Waters, Howlin' Wolf, and Otis Rush. These songs feel more appropriate for my emotional state than the revelry of big rock 'n' roll, and I never did go in for the pasty singer-songwriter thing.

There's a balance I try to strike with the streets I walk down: too busy or too quiet and I feel exposed, but a good side street with the occasional dog walker, smoker, or biking child gives me the sense of invisibility I need to calm my raw nerves. It's an uncannily beautiful afternoon, and the breeze smells like purple flowers. Every day since I've been out of treatment, I've told myself I'd finally stop by my apartment, but once again, I can't bring myself to do it. I can't face Mari, or the Virgen de Guadalupe, or the drawers of my dresser, where an assortment of pills are surely still stashed away. It isn't that I feel like using, particularly, but I assume the urge will come eventually, and that looming fear is more than I can handle.

I walk into the meeting ten minutes before it starts. This one is held in a room at the back of a Cuban coffee shop in Silver Lake, less than a mile from my apartment. Today's group is typical of the addicts in this part of town, mostly a mix of aging punk-rock guys and women with candy-colored hair, plus a handful of paperback-clutching off-track intellectuals thrown in for scenery. Everyone smells like an ashtray, different but no less appealing to me than that purple flora.

There's no guest speaker today, and the chairperson, a woman named Vivian who has an octopus tattooed all across her back and down her arms, starts the meeting with a rundown of official business—it seems someone keeps forgetting to bring the coffee cake.

The door swings open, and everyone turns to watch a man mumble an apology for being late. His face is flecked with scabs, and he's missing a tooth, just like me. He has to walk past our whole row of seats to get to the empty one on the end, making me feel almost like we're judging a pageant. He looks right into my eyes as he passes by, and I can tell he recognizes me but can't quite pinpoint where from.

But I know who he is.

"Blake," I mutter. Those eyes I used to daydream about are yellow and dull, that hair, once so deliberate, gone feral. He drops his gaze, but it doesn't matter. I already know everything about him. I know that the flames of hell have been licking at his boots each and every moment since the last time I saw him. I know he sold his camera and bought it back, then sold it again. I know he spent some time living on the street, nearly dying on the street, on his best days seeing only the fluorescent lights of purgatory illuminating the way in front of him. I know his insides are covered with a stain of methamphetamine no amount of scrubbing could ever hope to shoo away. And I know beyond a shadow of a doubt that he did some real, lasting damage to a teenage girl quite a few years ago.

Vivian reads a section from the Big Book that has the ring of lullaby. It's the way she says the words, solidly and like she believes them, more than the meaning itself that gives me a little peace. She closes the book and offers the floor to anyone who wants to share. I haven't spoken at a meeting yet, but today seems like a good time to start. I raise my hand, and Vivian nods at me. I stand. I can feel Blake watching me, but I don't look his way.

"I'm Leila," I say. "Addict and alcoholic. I've got thirty-five days clean, which is the longest stretch I've gone since I was in high school. The truth is, I don't know any other way to live. But it's occurred to me that I can probably learn one, right? What I mean is, it feels like I might actually be ready to change my life. But that's today, and tomorrow will be tomorrow. And we all know how hard it is to think about tomorrow."

The whole room claps for me, and I sit back down, already thinking of things I want to say the next time.

EXT. LEILA'S APARTMENT — AFTERNOON

Leila stands outside her apartment, hesitant. She takes
a deep breath and unlocks the door.

INT. LEILA'S APARTMENT — CONTINUOUS

Leila steps through the door and looks around.

                         LEILA
          Mari?

No response. She takes a step forward and yelps. Looks
down and sees a sticky mousetrap attached to her foot.

                         LEILA
          Damn it.

Leila removes her shoes and heads into her bedroom to
grab another pair.

She looks up at her Virgen de Guadalupe mural. She
traces the woman's features with her fingertip.

She looks over all her things and begins to pull
clothes from a drawer. She spots a package on the desk
and picks it up.

A note reads: "I fucking miss you. Take this and cut it
into little stars. Your Johnny."

Leila opens the package. Inside is a gram of black tar
heroin.

Leila looks at the drugs for a long time. She drops them on the desk and curls up into a fetal position on top of her unmade bed.

CHAPTER THIRTY-ONE

I walk into the house carrying a bunch of fresh-cut flowers. They're calla lilies, delicate and white and clean. My parents are making dinner together, whipping up a batch of pasta in a deep-red spicy tomato sauce. They both look up at me as soon as I enter, like they've been attuned to every single sound all evening.

"Hi," I say. I put the flowers in a vase and put the vase on the table.

"Hello, sweetheart," my mom says. We share a smile.

I see my father glance over at the flowers a few times in a row, and I realize I've forgotten to put water in the vase. He knows it too, but he lets it be.

"Can I help?" I ask.

"Let's get you on garlic bread duty," my dad says.

I slice a loaf of crusty Italian bread down the middle and spread butter up and down both halves. My dad hands me a clove of garlic, and I chop it into fine pieces. The three of us lose ourselves in the work for a minute, silent except for the sounds of cutting and washing.

"Hey," I say. "I was thinking—"

"Yes?" my mother asks too quickly.

"If there are leftovers, maybe tomorrow I'll invite Mari over for dinner?"

"That would be perfect," my mom says, smiling, and my father agrees.

EPILOGUE

INT. BEDROOM — MAGIC HOUR

Tight on a pair of lightly closed eyes. An abstract
mask of brown haze comes over them. Spots of color
dance the Charleston across both lids.

Pulling back, we see Leila, naked except for a pair
of lacy black underwear. She is slumped over, with
her face resting atop her arm, and completely still.
Slashes of golden light cut across her body.

Her lips are slightly parted, and the color has begun
to drain from her face. Her mouth, freshly rouged,
stands out against the paling skin. Her eyes appear
delicate and almost peaceful.

A lit cigarette crackles in a makeshift ashtray.

A flower sits in a tiny vase.

The perfect song plays.

So much stillness, so beautiful and poignant.

The mask of brown haze fills the frame, and it slowly
begins to darken, bleeding inward from the edges.
Darker and darker, until . . .

WE FADE TO BLACK.

ACKNOWLEDGMENTS

Firstly, I want to thank my family for having been the greatest and the most supportive people on earth for my entire life. Carol, Jack, and Dylan: I love you dummies.

There would, of course, be no book at all if not for the faith and input of my impossibly smart and way too lovely editor, Carmen Johnson.

And I owe a huge debt of gratitude to Melissa Kahn, Richard Abate, and Jermaine Johnson, all three of whom have been invaluably helpful and insightful throughout this entire process.

Thank you to Elizabeth Johnson, my copyeditor, for teaching me how to spell "Wookiee."

Richard Rushfield was the first person to read parts of this book in its most fetal form, and his feedback and encouragement gave me the resolve to keep going with it.

Stephanie Carroll has read more drafts than is reasonable to ask of a person, and she never even complained about it, because she is amazing.

Kevin Seccia said, "I like that book idea you told me about—why don't you just write that already" enough times that I eventually did.

And finally, along the way, some dear friends have offered various forms of support and encouragement that have meant more to me than they could ever know. Thank you to Aimee Mann, Ashley Cardiff, B. J. Novak, Bigfoot (that is my dog—shut up), Daniel O'Brien, Drew Grant, Jacob Pitts, Jarrett Grode, Jeremy Schoenherr, Maya Dean, Rob Delaney, Sarah Linet, Stephen Falk, Taylor Grode, and Tyler Coates.

ABOUT THE AUTHOR

Liana Maeby was born in Brooklyn and raised in Los Angeles, where she still lives. This is her first novel.